CREATIVE WOMAN MYSTERIES®

Guilty
Treasures

Rachael Phillips

Annie's®
AnniesFiction.com

Library of Congress-in-Publication Data
Guilty Treasures / by Rachael Phillips
p. cm.
I. Title
                    2013942050

AnniesFiction.com
(800) 282-6643
Creative Woman Mysteries
Series Editor: Shari Lohner

10 11 12 13 14 | Printed in China | 9 8 7 6 5 4 3 2

— Prologue —

Oregon Coast, February 1942

"**I**t's gold." Captain James Paisley stroked the coin's surface. His fingers tingled as they outlined the worn cross and lion stamped into tarnished metal. He'd spent months of wracking his brain, endlessly searching in the dark by flashlight, sometimes digging like a mole during the sea's cold, angry months—the only time when frolickers deserted the beach—but it couldn't steal the warmth pumping through him.

"Spanish doubloon, Cap'n?" His first mate's young eyes gleamed. Corny stretched a finger to touch the coin.

James squelched the urge to yank it away. "The real thing. Right era—late sixteenth century."

"How much is it worth?"

"Think I'd tell you?" James forced a smile and handed the doubloon to Corny.

The kid caressed it like the face of a long-lost love.

"OK, enough," James said. "After all that work, we'd better stick it someplace safe before we lose it."

"I'll keep it for you." Grinning, Corny pretended to pocket the doubloon.

James chuckled as he snatched the coin and deposited it

inside his coat. "After we're done, I'll buy you a hot-buttered rum. We can sit by a fire and admire the coin all night."

"Sounds great." Corny's smirk widened. "Even better if you keep the drinks comin', Cap'n."

"Count on it," James said, though even the best tavern euphoria couldn't match his sense of accomplishment right now. The shoreline crags had tried to hide Parable Rock, the crosslike formation, from him. His ancestor Angus Paisley had taunted him with cryptic clues; yet, with hard work, James had succeeded in solving the puzzle. He'd beaten Angus this round of the treasure-hunting game. He recited a clue aloud just for the pleasure of it: "'Christe Jesus told the story, yet He willna own the doubloon's glory, nor even a wee tithe of the treasure near.'"

Corny shook his head. "How did you memorize that stuff?"

"I've studied it enough."

"Strange clue, especially for your great-great-great-great-grandfather. Not exactly the religious type." Corny haw-hawed, his squinty blue eyes disappearing into rosy chapped cheeks. "Who woulda thought some dusty Sunday school story would help you find the right spot to dig?"

"Maybe the old pirate's father made him attend church when he was a boy." James reached into the pocket of his mackinaw and pulled out a copy of the map he'd sketched from the centuries-old original. "Now to find the treasure itself."

"Too bad Angus couldn't just mark the longitude and latitude where he hid the chest and be done with it." Corny shifted his brawny body to block the wind.

"Too smart for that." James had explained this before. "Corny, Angus *stole* from his captain, Sir Francis Drake. He had to fool Drake, his enemies, and probably his friends too. He couldn't make a map that would spell it out." He gripped the paper, flapping in the gale like an angry gull. "You game to explore Wild Woman Waters tonight?"

"What? Where those Indian caves are?" Corny's enthusiasm slipped another notch. "You think the treasure's *there*?"

"I do." James pointed to the bay on the map, a quarter mile away. "It fits the next clue:

'How canna forget the bonnie wench,
Witchy hair fallin' to her knee?
Strong lass a-dancin', soaper a-dancin',
Luve and gowld for me, but death to thee.'"

"At least he's not quotin' a Sunday School lesson in this one." Corny leaned on his shovel. "Can't we celebrate the coin tonight and explore the caves in daylight?"

"Too public, and you know it." James scoffed, "You'd let a few spooky Indian stories scare you away from the treasure?"

Something of his own flaming desire reignited that of his first mate. Corny stuck out his chin. "Ain't nothing going to keep me from finding that big ol' chest of gold."

"That's the spirit." James clapped the lad on the back. "With the draft on, we'd better find it fast …."

James let his words die. Corny stared at the roiling waves. The Japanese attack on Pearl Harbor just before last Christmas had blown the world apart. Now war threatened their quest.

So far, Corny had escaped shipping out on the troop trains. In his twenties, James knew his own seafaring skills might eventually land him in combat at some point, but right now both men had been exempted from conscription because their work on James's cargo ship was considered "essential services." Corny and James also had joined the local volunteer flotilla of fishermen who, night and day, kept a lookout for Japanese submarine activity.

"Maybe they'll keep us here, patrolling the coastline," Corny said.

"That would make too much sense," James joked, trying to lighten the moment. "We'll probably find ourselves in foxholes a thousand miles from the nearest water."

Corny guffawed—he never worried too long about anything—shouldered his shovel, and followed James south.

As they fought the wind, James tried not to imagine searching for the treasure without Corny's endless energy and camaraderie. Yet, if Corny were drafted, who would listen to James's hopes and share the torrid joy of the treasure? James preferred not to kindle treasure lust in his more intelligent friends.

Still, his first mate's inevitable departure might work out for the best.

Lately, Corny had shown far too much interest in the Paisley treasure.

— 1 —

Apple Grove, Oregon, present day

"**D**rinks are on me, ladies!" Melanie Burkhart's yell, as she burst into Espresso Yourself, stunned the Purls of Hope knitting circle. She might as well have tossed firecrackers into their cozy corner.

Shannon McClain, owner of the coffeehouse and the Paisley Craft Market that housed it, handed her friend her usual caramel macchiato. "Sit and tell us the good news, or we won't get anything done tonight." She looked closer at Melanie. The dark-haired, forty-something woman's thin face, usually pale and composed, flushed candy pink. "Are you all right?"

Joyce Buchanan, a plump, bling-y blonde, threw aside the purple argyle sock she was knitting and trumpeted into an imaginary game show microphone: "She's won a ten-year supply of gen-u-ine color-coordinated French designer vacuum cleaner bags!" Joyce woo-hooed and offered Melanie a fake congratulatory hug. "Isn't this wonderful, folks? No wonder she's so excited!"

Melanie half-sputtered, half-giggled, unable to speak.

Shannon rolled her eyes at Joyce. As Melanie quieted, Shannon coaxed her, "Go on. Tell us."

"Tell us!" Betty Russo and Kate Ellis clamored.

"I'm still cancer free!" Behind Melanie's glasses, tears

pooled in her green-sparkle eyes. "The doctor said my chance of a recurrence has dropped significantly now."

"Are you serious, girl?"

"Group hug, group hug!"

The Purls leaped from their chairs and scrummed in a joyous dance.

Shannon embraced the happy tremor of Melanie's shoulders. *Cancer. Ugly word.* God willing, Melanie would never have to say it again.

"Why didn't you tell us you had an appointment in Portland?" Betty finally demanded in a half-happy, half-aggravated motherly tone. "One of us could have gone with you."

Kate wiped her eyes. "Did Greg take time off to go with you?"

"No, I didn't want to bother him. My son's been through enough." Melanie raised her chin. "You've all been through enough."

"As if you haven't." Shannon patted her shoulder. Not only had breast cancer ravaged her friend, but Melanie's no-good husband had left her the minute he'd learned her diagnosis. Shannon shot a warning look at Joyce, whose blue eyes held a wicked glint. *Don't say you're glad he's dead.*

"I'm so, so happy for you." Joyce waltzed Melanie around the room. Shannon breathed a sigh of relief. Maybe Joyce's past struggles with false accusations had taught her not to verbalize *everything*.

Shannon concocted another round of drinks, on the house. No way would she allow Melanie to pay for these. She wondered if life could get any better. Such incredible, loyal friends. While the Purls of Hope knit yarns into warm socks, hats, and throws for the needy, they also knit their lives into a friendship that never unraveled. Fiftyish Betty Russo, who owned The Apple Grove Inn with her husband, Tom, kept the Purls on track with her down-to-earth approach and a smile that brightened any situation. Kate Ellis, a dog lover, channeled kindheartedness into her business, Ultimutt Grooming, as well as into her friends. Melanie, a florist at the Flower Pot, said little but did much to support the other Purls. And dear, mouthy Joyce, the owner of Pink Sprinkles Bakery, gladly would have tossed her last coconut cream pie into the face of their enemy.

Though Shannon missed her twins, Lara and Alec, they enjoyed their classes at Portland State, and she was learning to channel her energies into her specialties: silversmithing and beadwork. Both her craft market and coffee shop had posted growing profits in the past year, and several prominent artists rented studios in her loft.

And, yes, her face grew warm when she thought of Hunter, who had come to Apple Grove to conduct marine research along the Oregon coast. Hunter, with his California surfer looks and sunlit smile, had brightened her world, reminding her how much she loved life.

Her phone rang. Lara? Hunter? She set the whipped cream on the granite counter and turned so the chattering Purls wouldn't see as she slipped her cell from her khakis pocket.

It was Deborah, her housekeeper. A ripple of disappointment disturbed the perfect flow of the moment.

Hunter doesn't have to call every day, Shannon admonished herself. *We haven't been dating that long.* She tapped the phone. "Deborah. What's up?"

No response.

"Hello?" Shannon checked the screen. Still connected?

"Oh, Shannon."

Fire alarms shrilled in her head. Her take-charge employee and friend never sounded this agitated. "What's wrong? Are you sick? Did the twins call?"

"No, no … but …."

"Tell me, dear." Shannon bit her lip. "Quick."

"Someone broke in."

"Broke in?" Shannon choked on the words. The Purls' joyous henfest quieted, and they all stared at her as she stuttered into her phone, "A-are you all right?"

"I'm OK. But I can't remember if I set the alarm before I went shopping," Deborah wailed.

"Don't even think about it right now—"

A whisper-scream. "I think I hear the intruder—he's still inside!"

"Lock yourself in the bathroom—"

"I did. I called 911."

"Try and stay calm. I'll be there in a minute." Shannon hung up and flung off her apron.

So much for her perfect life.

*   *   *

"Please don't go in there, Shannon." Deborah's voice trembled. She clutched a large, outdated flashlight. For the first time, Shannon's energetic white-haired housekeeper looked old.

Trying to shrug off Deborah's concern, Shannon crept toward the foyer's grand staircase. She raised the poker she'd grabbed from the library fireplace. "The guy's probably gone, but if he's stupid enough to hang around, I'll make him wish he hadn't."

She slipped down a side hall to the back staircase. The door to the closet built under it stood wide open. Shannon inhaled whiffs of cedar as she ducked inside and pushed aside parkas that had fallen to the floor. She dodged skis and poles crisscrossed at crazy angles. The intruder had slid aside a panel in a sidewall of the closet, revealing a large hidden door that resembled a bank vault's entrance, complete with a large combination lock. It, too, stood open. Neither she nor Deborah—who had worked at the Paisley mansion for decades—had ever seen it before.

"I wonder what my grandparents kept in here?" Shannon whispered as she crept closer.

"Wait till the police come," Deborah pleaded.

And let Chief Grayson wall me off from the crime scene in my own house? She almost wished Deborah hadn't called 911. Shannon edged forward, sharp end of the poker pointed straight ahead.

She stopped just inside the vault's entrance. The cedar aroma gave way to an aged, papery smell, as if the tiny room had been sealed for years. For a moment, Shannon's lungs threatened to fold like fans, and she wanted to run from the close, cramped space. Instead, she focused on the dark cave before her. In the dim light, she detected no movement. No place to hide either. "He's gone, Deborah. Hand me the flashlight."

Shannon swept the secret room with the strong beam of light. Spider webs shrouded every corner. She scanned the dust-coated wooden floor with the beam again. Footprints!

Smooshed together as the burglar moved around, but clear enough to compare to her own feet. Much larger. Probably a man's.

What was he after?

Prickles of fear beaded her spine, but Shannon gave herself a pep talk. *These are like footprints in the snow. They'll help lead us to whoever did this.*

Shannon peered at shadowy rows of old books on shelves. Fuzzy miniatures of sailing ships gave the room a seaworthy feel. An antique compass and other navigational-looking instruments added to the effect. They probably could bring high prices. Why hadn't the thief taken them? Or had Deborah scared him off before he could steal them?

Shannon hated the thought of breathing the stale air, yet she longed to investigate. If she did proceed any farther, though, she might destroy evidence.

Would she even show the secret room to the police chief? She hadn't decided. Shannon pointed the flashlight at a small desk facing the wall, the only furniture in the small space. It had three drawers, one with a lock that looked as if someone had tampered with it. An empty kerosene lamp sat on top.

A chiming bell interrupted her inspection. *Blast.*

Shannon left the door open a tiny crack and slid the panel shut. While she pushed skis and poles against it, she called to Deborah, "Stall Grayson in the foyer!"

"Are you insane?" For a moment, Deborah sounded like herself. "Aren't you going to tell—"

"I'm not sure." Shannon hastily hung up coats.

The doorbell, pushy as the police chief himself could

be at times, demanded an answer. Shannon heard Deborah greet him. She played the frightened female with a quaver in her voice. Or maybe she wasn't acting? Shannon exited the closet and shut the door, scolding herself for ignoring her friend's trepidation. She brushed her clothes and hurried to the mansion's foyer.

Grayson, his thinning hair sticking up, was examining the front entrance keypad. She heard him mumble, "Perp must have been wearing gloves." Grayson hardly glanced at Shannon as he instructed one policeman to search inside. Officer Brownley nodded to her sympathetically before he and another officer split up to search the estate's yard and adjoining acreage. Grayson's right-hand man was a polite young fellow who didn't overstep his authority.

"Let's nail this down." Grayson's dark eyes bored into Deborah's red-rimmed ones. "The front door was standing open when you came home—unusual during a theft, but this house sits a long distance from the road, behind all these trees. Tell me, did you turn on the security system earlier, before you left the house?"

Shannon joined them. "May I fix Deborah a cup of tea? I'm sure she'll answer your questions with more clarity when she's recovered a bit."

Grayson bristled. As usual, he reminded Shannon of a temperamental bulldog. "First impressions are important. I want to get the facts down before she forgets them—"

"I'm not senile yet, thank you very much." A spark of Deborah's usual moxie flashed at him.

"But you may have forgotten to turn on the alarm?" Grayson asked.

Deborah wilted. "Yes."

"I forget occasionally too," Shannon said, wanting to reassure her housekeeper, who was wringing the hem of her sensible cardigan as if it were soaked.

Grayson's phone rang, and he growled into it. "Any sign of the perp?"

He barked more instructions, then turned back to them and said, "It looks like the guy rummaged through a couple of closets—one in the basement and one upstairs. No sign of him, though."

Shannon waited for him to say more. *Should that make us feel better?*

Grayson demanded, "If you forgot to turn on the alarm, how did the intruder know that?" He paused. "If you did turn on the alarm, how did he get past the security system?"

How, indeed? Michael Stone, a top-of-the-line security expert, had redesigned the system when a burglar had broken in soon after Shannon inherited the beautiful old house.

Grayson made valid points. She didn't like to think about the implications behind his words.

She also didn't like to think about Michael.

"I'm sorry, Chief Grayson." Deborah's quiet voice brought Shannon back to the present. Her housekeeper still clutched her sweater, but she lifted her chin. "I don't remember. I do know that I locked the door with my key. I hate all these gadgets and gizmos. From now on, though, I'll certainly pay more attention to them."

From the set of her mouth, Shannon knew Deborah meant what she said. *Look out, burglar. She may take a rolling pin to you next time.*

Grayson grunted. "Have you noticed anything missing?"

"Not yet," Shannon said truthfully. She didn't yet know if anything had been taken from the secret room.

"Check your belongings while I go over your security system, but touch stuff only if you have to. If you see anything odd, back off. Come and get me."

Yes, sir! Shannon wanted to salute him. Probably not a good idea.

She gestured to Deborah. "Would you check downstairs while I go up?"

The housekeeper's eyes darted toward the back closet. Shannon gave a miniscule shake of her head. *Don't tell him.*

Deborah blew out a nervous breath and headed for the dining room. Shannon hoped the intruder hadn't raided her Grandmother Victoria's silver, more for Deborah's sake than for her own. Shannon hadn't known her grandmother personally, so replacing it via insurance payment would not pain her deeply. She even let herself fantasize about designing new pieces. In Deborah's eyes, however, no new set, no matter how gorgeous, could replace the silver she had polished for decades while working for Victoria.

Going upstairs presented more of a challenge than Shannon anticipated. A thousand tiny hairs rose on her arms as she reached the top.

Don't be a wimp. The guy was gone. The officer said so. Shannon made herself check Lara's room, then Alec's. Lara's closet, stuffed with clothes, hadn't been touched, whereas Alec's sparse summer wardrobe and a few outgrown coats lay on his closet floor. Grayson had said the intruder had also searched a basement closet. Why do that, with plenty of expensive items in plain view?

Thank heaven, the kids had taken their electronics to college. Even if the guy had stolen Shannon's computer and external backup, she kept copies of everything in her store computer. Not much else upstairs a burglar would want, except the antique paintings on the hallway walls. He probably hadn't had time to grab those.

She hesitated outside her own door, not wanting to know if the creep had stolen her jewelry. Fortunately, she kept the exquisite locket that had triggered her American adventure in her bank's lockbox. But what about her pearls? She couldn't bear parting with the necklace her late husband, John, had fastened around her neck the Christmas before he died, or the tiny pearl earrings he'd given her as a bride. A familiar sweet ache brought back their wedding, with John so handsome in his clan's plaids ....

What if the burglar had made off with her rings? Her heartbeats thundered in her ears. After several years of widowhood, she'd only recently removed them from her hand.

Shannon bared her teeth at the thief. *You may have stolen my jewelry, but you can't steal my memories.*

She marched into her bedroom. Her white leather jewelry case sat on her dresser. She jiggled its clasp. Locked. She slipped the key from its hiding place in the closet and opened the case. The plain gold band and the ice-chip diamond in Shannon's engagement ring glimmered from their satiny cushions.

She leaned against the wall, limp with relief. Within seconds, though, she stiffened and ran to her nightstand. She yanked open the drawer.

"Yesss!" Her almost-completed bead project, a mosaic hanging of Joseph wearing his coat of many colors, had not been sullied. Shannon hugged it to her chest, then unfolded it. She pressed the beads to her cheek, savoring their knobby comfort.

She wished she could hold the hanging forever, but she made herself place it back in her nightstand. Shannon searched the rest of the room, even checked under the massive canopy bed she'd inherited, though she couldn't think of a good reason why. Nothing missing.

"Shannon? Are you all right up there?" Deborah's voice floated up the stairs.

"I'm fine." Shannon scurried from the room and headed for the first floor. Deborah met her on the landing and wrapped her in a rare hug.

"So far as I can see, the guy took only those little marble Peruvian statues and the bronze vase from the foyer." Deborah's no-nonsense voice had returned. Her arms loosened their grip on Shannon, then dropped to her sides. "Not terribly bright of him, given all the valuable things your grandmother collected."

"Nothing's missing upstairs." Shannon smiled a little. "For that, we can be thankful."

They checked the basement together, then reported to Chief Grayson. He seemed almost annoyed that he'd devoted his afternoon to a thief who took so little. He sent his officers on other assignments via his phone, then asked Shannon, "Anybody know the security code besides you two?"

"My twins, of course."

He snorted. "College kids, right?"

"This is their home," Shannon snapped.

"And they have lots of friends, don't they? Friends who come here on weekends, stay here so they can go to the beach?" A note of sarcasm edged his voice. "Friends who may have gotten locked out at some point and begged for the code?"

Shannon ached to tell Grayson about the secret room, if for no other reason than to say, "This has nothing to do with my children or their friends. You're wrong, wrong, wrong."

But was he?

2

Shannon managed to endure Grayson's questions and safety lecture without spilling her secret. The moment he left, she darted past her late grandmother's enormous Roman horse statue and the grand staircase, zipping down the hallway to the back stairway closet. Deborah followed on her heels and helped Shannon shove aside the coats and winter equipment. She grabbed a camera hanging from a hook, donned thin gloves, and slid the secret panel open.

Deborah handed Shannon the flashlight again. "I'm not sure you should have kept this from Grayson."

"It's my house." Shannon knew she sounded petulant, like territorial Lara at fourteen. "I wanted to examine the room myself. He wouldn't have let me near it."

Quickly, Shannon swung the door open and inspected the room—more closely this time. She hadn't noticed the undisturbed strip of dust on the floor in front of the bookcase before. The perfect path inside. She could stand there and study the room without destroying any footprint evidence, if she were careful. Shannon stuck her head outside the closet and took deep, un-dusty breaths. Then she handed the flashlight back to Deborah, readied the camera, and tiptoed inside.

"Where do you want me to point this?" Deborah asked, holding the flashlight high.

"Right where you've got it is perfect."

Shannon photographed the floor, the bookcase with its tomes and relics, and the desk. She hung the camera around her neck and stretched her gloves taut. Carefully digging her fingers into both sides of the desk drawer with the jimmied lock, she pulled it open and flicked on her phone for more light.

Inside she found additional layers of dust and little else— an old-fashioned brass letter opener, ink-stained fountain pens, and scattered rusty paper clips. But a small rectangular outline in the drawer's bottom captured her attention.

The intruder had removed something.

A book? If so, it was much smaller than a paperback.

A jewelry box perhaps?

"Find anything in there?"

Deborah's voice nearly sent Shannon through the ceiling. Her housekeeper stood at the door, holding the flashlight, craning her neck.

Feeling silly for being so jumpy, Shannon said, "I found something that's not here." She gestured. "Come and look, but please stay close to the bookcase. We don't want to mess up any footprints."

"You know I won't touch anything I shouldn't," Deborah grumbled. But she complied, then squinted at the outline in the open drawer. "The guy seemed to know what he was looking for."

Shannon nodded, a chill threading through her. "Would you hold the flashlight higher?" She opened the other drawers. Empty. Lightly tapping the underside and outer walls of each drawer, she checked for secret compartments.

Nothing.

Deborah's lips tightened. "Are you sure you should be doing this?"

Shannon turned away from her housekeeper's frown. "If only I could move this desk—"

Ding-dong.

Shannon grimaced. "I'd love to pretend we're not home. But Grayson may be back." She steered Deborah through the door, turned, and closed it partway again.

"Maybe it's the plumber," Deborah said. "About time. I called him three days ago, when the kitchen drains started running slow." She maneuvered her way out of the closet and headed for the foyer.

Shannon repeated the camouflage routine and shut the closet door, then she halted.

The male voice that rumbled from the entrance wasn't Grayson's. Or a plumber's.

Michael.

Of course. He monitored his police scanner 24/7. Or so it seemed.

In her will, Shannon's grandmother had hired Michael to protect her during her first turbulent year in America, but that didn't make it a lifetime commitment— er, assignment.

Why had he come? Michael had communicated their non-relationship status quite clearly after their one and only disastrous date.

Shannon hung the last coat, smoothed her hair and slowed her steps to the foyer. She stopped behind the horse statue and listened.

"Coffee while you're waiting?" Deborah asked, her voice sounding unusually strained.

"No, thanks."

Shannon had to admit that Michael had come to her aid time and time again with his expertise and resources— even saved her life on more than one occasion. The stress of the whole situation was making her cranky. She arranged a smile on her face and sauntered forward. "Oh, hello."

"Hi."

Deborah gave Shannon a pointed look and bustled off, leaving them to stare at each other.

Thanks a lot, friend. Shannon kept the smile, but she struggled for words. All she wanted to do was sprint back to the secret room and investigate.

Michael finally spoke. "I heard you had some trouble today."

"Yes. A burglary while Deborah was shopping."

"Security system on?"

"Deborah's not sure she activated it."

If only he wouldn't look at her like that. Michael's cobalt eyes pierced through Shannon as if dissecting her thoughts. Hunter's, on the other hand, were a warm, twinkly green, like a brook on a sunny day ....

"Maybe I should check it out." Michael's curt tones interrupted her pleasant mini-reverie. He held up the investigative kit he kept with him.

She wanted to refuse, but Michael knew more about the system than Grayson. "OK. I'll be working upstairs if you need me."

She'd longed for time to experiment with new bead

patterns, but a break-in hardly fostered creativity. Instead, she worked at her bedroom computer, buried in accounts and inventories, trying to forget Michael was near, forget about the secret room—and that some faceless trespasser knew her house better than she did.

*   *   *

"The security system looks as good as the day I installed it."

Michael didn't sound defensive. As always, he simply stated facts. "Any ideas about who did this?"

Shannon felt as if his intense gaze were pinning her to her chair at the breakfast table. She wished she had decided beforehand how much to tell him. "Um, Grayson asked about the twins' college friends."

Michael said nothing, only looking at her.

Shannon babbled on, "He's probably right. Of course, I told the twins never to share the code, but with all the coming and going, especially last summer's craziness—"

"I'm not asking what Grayson thinks. He's a good cop, but you usually come up with your own ideas."

A corner of his mouth twitched. Was he hiding a grin? Heat crept up Shannon's face. "I can't picture any of those kids breaking into my house. Some need money. But they know I would help if they asked."

"I'm sure they do."

Was it her imagination, or did he lean forward a little? Shannon tried not to draw back. "Sure you wouldn't like coffee?"

"I'm sure."

Not her imagination. Michael bent an inch closer. "Any way I can help?"

You can help by leaving. Shannon sipped the chai tea Deborah had fixed. "I'm sure you're very busy."

"Of course I am. But I'm not leaving until you tell me whatever it is you're hiding."

She choked on the chai and half-gurgled, "Perhaps you should mind your own business."

Silence.

She hated his silences. They felt so deliberate, calculated to make people spill their guts. Yet, part of her craved his help. She dreaded the coming night, lying in her grandmother's huge canopy bed, listening in the black hole of quiet for creaking stairs, menacing footsteps approaching her room—

"All right. All right." Shannon wanted to dump her chai on him, but she gulped the last few drops instead. "I'll show you what we found. But don't breathe a word about it to anyone."

What a stupid thing to say. Michael was, first and foremost, a discreet professional. She dared cast a glance toward him. No gloating in his neutral expression. He hid everything. More annoyed than ever, Shannon rose. He followed her to the back stairway.

They encountered Deborah in the hall. *You're going to show him?* her sour expression asked. Nevertheless, she fetched the old flashlight for them.

Shannon opened the closet door, yanked the coats aside, and dragged out the ski equipment.

Michael stacked it all next to the wall without a word.

She slid the left sidewall panel open, pulled the heavy door ajar, and turned to him, her arms crossed. His eyes widened.

Shannon said, "I had no idea this existed. Neither did Deborah, until she found it like this."

"Mind if I take a look?" No neutrality in Michael's expression now. If he'd been a German shepherd, his ears would have stood at attention.

She gestured with her head. "The extra footprints are Deborah's and mine."

He slipped in—how could a man that large move so fast? Much as she longed to examine the room and its contents, she didn't follow. Michael filled the space—no need to get up close and snuggly with him.

He whipped out a small but powerful flashlight and scanned the room. Then he slipped on gloves, using a delicate touch in his investigation when moving something was necessary. She was glad to see him dust for fingerprints. His camera would take much better photos than hers. He measured and mumbled.

When his movements finally slowed, Shannon asked, "OK if I take a turn?"

"So that's why you didn't tell Grayson about it." He said it as a statement, not a question.

She nodded. "I wanted to examine it before anyone else did."

"Sorry to have crashed your party." He didn't look sorry as he exited the room and began tinkering with the vault door's lock.

She sniffed. "Some party." He was right, though. The old books, ships, and the desk made her salivate almost as much as Deborah's Death by Chocolate Cake.

As if he'd read her mind, Michael said, "I've gathered as much evidence as I can. Do whatever you want."

Thanks for your permission. Shannon walked in and slid a large book from the bookcase's first row. A small black book fell out, a child's New Testament. Her irritation at Michael drained away.

Shannon picked up the large book and carefully turned its yellowed pages. "This looks like a ship's log." While Michael made notes and collected his tools, she skimmed the first entries, excitement washing over her. "These are signed by Captain James Paisley. My grandfather."

She examined the Testament. Wobbly letters in the front told her it once had belonged to James and that his father had given it to him.

To see her grandfather's childhood Bible, to hold a book full of notes in his cramped, faded handwriting ... She hadn't cried when her house was burglarized. Now, though, surprise tears clung to her eyelashes.

She drove his ridiculous old truck, the one her artistic grandmother had kept after his death, despite its eye-popping shade of blue. But she'd never seen his writing. Until now.

Shannon didn't realize how much time had passed until Michael touched her elbow. He said, "Looks like you have plenty of reading material."

Sniffling, Shannon nodded. "This nautical stuff is Chinese to me. I'll find someone to analyze it." She struggled to sound businesslike. "James also listed his work schedule, appointments and so forth. Perhaps I'll find a clue as to when and why he built this room, why he kept it a secret—"

"And why somebody knew about it and broke into it."

Michael's clipped but urgent tones brought her thoughts back to the burglary. He said, "You should update this lock immediately. We know the intruder stole something from this room—and little else, despite the wealth of salable objects available—but we don't know if he found all he was looking for. I'll email you contact information for locksmiths who design almost infallible safe mechanisms."

At her nod, he continued, "I'll run an analysis on my findings immediately. I probably can call you with some results by tomorrow night."

"I—I'll be gone tomorrow night." Though Michael had her cell number, Shannon didn't want him to call. Tomorrow, she had a date with Hunter. "I'll call you before work the next morning, OK?"

"Sure." His face and voice morphed to neutral again. "You might check with your mother and see if she knows about this room. Even if she doesn't, she knew your grandfather and might be able to help fill in some holes."

Of course. Beth would know better than anyone. Thankfulness refreshed Shannon's murky uncertainty. She'd lived without a mother for so many years that she sometimes forgot Beth lived nearby, in Portland.

"In the meantime, be careful," Michael warned. "Keep this room's existence a secret. Re-program a new code into your system, and don't share it with anyone other than Deborah. No one."

Her hackles rose at his tone. Shannon flushed. Did he seriously think she might give her door code to Hunter?

He continued, "Maybe Beth or a friend can stay with you and Deborah. The more the merrier. Staying overnight alone isn't an option. Talk to you soon."

He turned and left before she could form a coherent reply.

Still steaming, she yanked out her phone and called Beth.

3

"Of *course* I came." Sparks flew from Beth's eyes as Shannon held open the mansion's back door. "How could you think otherwise?"

Beth dropped a duffle bag and enfolded Shannon in her arms so tightly she could feel Beth's heart throb against her own.

"But you need the business—"

"Not nearly as much as I need to know you're safe. Besides, I have capable employees."

Though Beth's words held a mom's firmness, uncertainty flitted in and out of her small smile.

Shannon eyed the duffle bag at her mom's feet. She obviously planned to spend the night. Shannon picked up the duffle. "Where would you like to stay?"

"In my old room, if that's OK—next to you."

"Would you like to see the secret room first?" Shannon couldn't mask her eagerness.

"Would I ever."

At the sight of the vault-room, Beth's jaw dropped. To Shannon's surprise, she didn't touch anything. She stood in the middle of the room, her mouth working, eyes opaque like green jade.

Shannon edged inside, reached for the New Testament, and handed it to Beth. "Look, your father's first Bible, I'll bet."

Her mother's eyes widened. She opened the little book's front cover.

Shannon pulled out the ship's log and gently turned the first pages. "This is one of Grandfather's captain's logs. See, he was sailing off the Oregon Coast before you were born, transporting goods from town to town."

Beth nodded as if she'd climbed aboard a dream. "He captained trips across the Pacific too, but Mom always said the short journeys kept us fed."

Shannon expected Beth to grab James's log or one of the shelved books, but she remained rooted.

Why the silence? Concern and tiny pins of irritation pierced Shannon's excitement.

Deborah stuck her nose in. "Before you two bury yourselves in there, come eat some chicken pot pie."

Though Shannon wanted to stay, her stomach growled a loud affirmative.

The sound seemed to break the spell over Beth. "Nothing like a burglary to stimulate an appetite." She returned the New Testament to the shelf.

"You both need something in your stomachs to help you handle this." Deborah eyed Shannon.

"All right. Supper first, mystery later."

Shannon followed them to the breakfast nook, where her favorite comfort food steamed invitingly. Six sparkling windows showed off the estate's still-lush lawn and fluttery golden aspens against dark evergreens. The beauty of her grandmother's artistic perspective in every room never failed to amaze her. If Shannon had planned the breakfast nook herself, she would have designed it the exact same way, with the exact same view.

They all talked and even laughed during their meal. Beth shared the latest news about the twins. Delighted at having a grandmother for the first time, especially so close by, Lara and Alec visited her often.

An hour away, Shannon had been struggling with their camaraderie. Seeing her children's happiness, though, she'd learned to welcome it.

The tired lines around Beth's mouth softened as she bragged about the twins' academic prowess. Shannon watched the metamorphosis with a flash of pleasure. She and Beth had come a long way since Shannon first learned her mother had disappeared only to protect her from the Camorra, the Scottish underworld that Beth, as a journalist, had exposed.

Now that the shock of the secret room had worn off, perhaps they could grow even closer in talking about Grandfather Paisley. He didn't often come up in their topics of conversation.

Stirring her Earl Grey, Shannon said, "I love driving Grandfather's truck, though sometimes Old Blue's as reliable as the weather."

Deborah sniffed. "Someday, that thing is going to quit on you halfway up a mountain."

"I've had it serviced several times. Old Blue runs well. It just doesn't like to wake up in the morning." Shannon grinned. "I wouldn't either, if I were that old—"

"Let's watch the remarks about getting old." Beth grimaced. "Old Blue is younger than me!"

"I was speaking in truck years, of course." Shannon patted her mother's hand. "Bombing around in Grandfather's favorite jalopy makes him seem a bit closer." Glancing at both women, she ventured, "Maybe it's crazy, but in a way, I'm grateful to the burglar."

Beth stared, china cup halfway to her mouth.

"Good grief, *why*?" Deborah pretended to feel Shannon's forehead for fever.

"I might not have discovered Grandfather's secret room otherwise. Now, with all these books and things, I'll understand him better." She leaned forward. "What was he like?"

"Like a hero out of a novel," Deborah answered. "Big, handsome, with all that straight, blond hair. Had a temper too."

Shannon slapped a hand to her jaw in mock surprise. "*None* of the Paisleys have tempers."

Deborah chuckled. "No comment. When he was in a mood, I made myself scarce. He was a brave, brave man, though."

"Even wearing a suit, like in the dining room portrait, he seems the swashbuckling type." Shannon wished she could have spent even one day with her grandparents.

"Apple Grove looked up to him as a World War II hero." Beth poured herself more tea from the blue-and-white Chinese pot. "I wasn't born until afterward, but whenever Father took Mom and me into town, he wore his Navy uniform, which made him seem even bigger than life. People always commented about the amazing way he outmaneuvered Japanese submarines." She smiled, but her eyes had assumed the blank look again. "His job took him away a lot, and he was lost at sea when I was little. I really didn't know him at all."

We can get better acquainted with him together. Shannon wanted to say it, but her mother remained quiet. Maybe the danger to Shannon kept Beth from seeing the secret room as positive. She'd certainly feel that way if someone had invaded the twins' dorm rooms.

Shannon wouldn't back down though. Nothing—not danger, not even Beth's apathy—would keep her away from that room tonight.

*　　　*　　　*

James's grimy ship tools looked incongruous in Shannon's study and craft room, decorated in feminine pastels as her Grandmother Victoria had left it. But bringing the antique collection out of the cavelike secret room had proved to be the right move. The seadog stuff on the big craft table seemed to awaken something in her mother.

"Sometimes, as a special treat, Father showed me this compass." A smile curved across Beth's face as she ran a finger around the worn brass case. "This wiggly needle fascinated me when I was a wee bairn."

Shannon blinked at the Scottish brogue that surfaced in Beth's thoroughly American speech. Besides her Scottish heritage, though, Beth had spent years in that country as a young woman—long enough to attend the University of St. Andrews, marry, and give birth to Shannon. At times, Shannon almost forgot that link.

She slid an arm around her mother, glad that a tender memory gleamed through Beth's foggy mood. "I've never understood how compasses work. Did Grandfather explain?"

"No." Beth replaced it on the table.

Shannon ached to explore the mysteries of the secret room's desk. Perhaps her mother knew something about her father's valuables and how he hid them. Given Beth's sudden reticence, though, Shannon wondered if she should wait until tomorrow before suggesting they explore James's hidden chamber.

Beth stared at the instruments again. Finally, she fingered a complicated-looking instrument with a short telescope, mirrors, metal arms, and clamps.

Shannon hesitated, then asked, "Do you know what that is?"

"A sextant. Years ago, captains used them to determine latitude and longitude."

"This spyglass looks really old." Shannon caressed its wood and tarnished silver.

"I once heard Father say his granddad had handed it down to him. He came from a long line of seafarers."

"What would he say about his landlubber granddaughter?" Shannon chuckled. "I get so seasick that I haven't gone whale watching since I moved here."

"I've never been a sailor either."

That odd blank expression lit in Beth's eyes again. Shannon hastened to keep her talking. She swept a hand to include the other instruments. "You've seen all these before?"

"I vaguely remember them. Father kept his favorite things here. This room was his library—strictly off-limits while he was at sea. Occasionally, when home, he invited me in and told me stories about his adventures." Beth looked away. "Later, I remember nosing around, but all the fun gadgets had disappeared. I never saw them again ... until now."

"Perhaps that's when Grandfather built the secret vault-room."

"Perhaps." Beth touched the compass again. "I recall my mother and I took a long trip to California around that time."

Just mentioning the secret room whetted Shannon's investigative appetite. She blurted, "I think the burglar stole something from Grandfather's desk—one of the drawers was forced open. Do you have any idea what it might have been?"

Beth didn't answer the question. Instead, she said, "You're dying to check out that desk again, aren't you?"

Shannon flushed. Beth had read her like—like a mother. "Don't feel like you have to come with me."

"I don't. But I will." Beth stood. "Let's do it before you pop."

*   *   *

Shannon showed Beth the rectangular outline in the jimmied drawer.

"Maybe the thief took a small jewelry box," her mother suggested. "Occasionally, Father brought back a ring or bracelet for my mother and trinkets for me, especially before I started school." Her voice flattened. "Or he could have hoarded jewels, waiting for just the right buyer."

"Perhaps he was saving for your future." Shannon wished Beth could think well of Grandfather. But then, Shannon herself hadn't accepted Beth at first.

She tried to shift the desk away from the wall. The old relic was much heavier than she'd anticipated.

"I'll help." Beth grasped the other end, and they created enough space between it and the wall for Shannon to examine the back of the desk. With Beth holding the flashlight, Shannon probed the edges where the back and sides intersected. She discovered a tiny crack. Taking the letter opener from the drawer, she gently inserted it into the gap.

The back panel slid open a quarter, then half an inch.

"What on earth …?" Beth's voice trailed away.

Blood pounding in her ears, Shannon slowly pushed it open to reveal a wide, thin space.

Empty.

She wanted to clobber the thief with Deborah's big black spider skillet. Shannon said dully, "If there was something here, it's gone now."

"I'm sorry, sweetheart." Beth almost crooned the words.

Her mother's voice echoed deep in the well of Shannon's memory, along with the pain of concrete smacking her knee and the grief of losing her one-eyed teddy bear.

She loved Beth's arm encircling her. But this time, her mother couldn't make it all better.

*   *   *

Hot, steaming cocoa. Triple whipped cream. They all needed it.

Shannon tried to lighten the evening with toasty time by the fire in her study. Scrabble distracted the other two from the mystery dumped on them that day.

Shannon, however, couldn't fathom waiting until tomorrow to read Grandfather's logs. While Deborah and Beth competed fiercely, Shannon schemed to read logs after bedtime.

Beth finally triumphed. Shannon congratulated her. Deborah made only a token attempt. As they headed toward the stairway, the housekeeper removed a .22 rifle from a closet and loaded it. She said, "I wish you'd let me teach you how to shoot properly."

Shannon, who'd endured this drill before, sighed. "That's not necessary—"

"This isn't our first break-in." Buckskins and a cowboy hat would have matched the gun Deborah carried better than her fluffy blue robe.

Shannon took a deep breath. "I know. But one loaded gun around the place is enough."

Quite enough. She'd never seen Deborah shoot it, and she didn't want to.

With a "Humph!" Deborah clomped toward her room, gun in hand.

Shannon didn't expect a similar scenario when Beth retired. She met Shannon in the hallway after she'd brushed her teeth. "Here, take one."

Shannon stared at the baseball bats Beth offered, no doubt borrowed from Alec's room. "Isn't this a little much?"

"After a burglary? No." She handed Shannon one, plus a can of pepper spray. "I keep one of these in my car at all times. I've lived in rough neighborhoods. I slept better when I took precautions."

Rather than argue, Shannon accepted the weapons, hugged Beth goodnight, and walked to her room, trying not to shake her head.

When the old mansion began its usual creaky lullaby, however, she began to think Deborah and Beth might be right. Darkness closed in, and the sly fall wind scratched branches against her windows. She could hear Beth snoring next door. Shannon climbed down from the huge bed twice, sure she heard someone downstairs. But if that were the case, surely he would have encountered Deborah, a light sleeper, and her .22 by now.

Hmm.

Maybe messing around in the secret room tonight hadn't been a good idea. Shannon slapped her pillow, then kneaded her neck muscles. She should have brought some of James's logs to bed with her.

Frustration kept her eyes wide open, but she knew computer work would only intensify her insomnia. She wasn't in the mood for the best-selling thriller on her nightstand. Besides, she'd already given in to her bad habit of reading the ending first.

Shannon rolled out of bed to check the windows and nearly swallowed her tongue when she spotted headlights following the long driveway from the road. When they reached the mansion's well-lit entrance, she drew a sigh of relief. A police car. Apparently Officer Brownley was keeping his promise to patrol the estate frequently. Surely the intruder wouldn't be stupid enough to return tonight. If he did, he'd find weapons awaiting him and fierce women wielding them.

As she watched the car's taillights shrink to red pinpoints and disappear into the surrounding woods, a welcome haze settled over her brain. Her eyelids drooped ... until a tiny movement at the edge of the house caught her eye.

Her imagination gibbered a thousand nightmares into the darkness. Her terrified bladder demanded she hide in the bathroom. She ignored both. Dropping to her knees, Shannon crept to the far window. Slowly she raised her head and peered over the windowsill.

Nothing.

Her wait seemed to last for hours. Still, nothing.

Call 911. Let the police check it out.

Not yet. Did she really want to awaken Grayson in the wee hours about a killer raccoon? Besides, even if the chief caught a real prowler, he'd tell her nothing. If he didn't catch the guy, he'd tell her nothing. Nevertheless, she grabbed her phone from the nightstand and stuck it in her hoodie pajama pocket.

Forget a bathroom break. Holding her knees together, she wobbled back to the window, never moving her gaze from the telltale spot.

Nothing.

The shadows shifted again.

A human-shaped shadow slithered out of her view. She quickly padded into the hall. The wall-rattling snores from Beth's room across the hall reassured her as she took her surveillance to Alec's bedroom window. The boy kept things neat. She'd risk her life crawling through Lara's room without lights.

Another century of waiting, watching. Breezes from the nearby Pacific swayed branches and feathery pine boughs in an effort to fool her.

Finally, she saw another movement, like a giant moth's, in the thickest brush. Shannon pulled out her phone.

Then she pushed it back into her pocket.

If I can move just a little closer ....

She slipped down the stairs, skipping the fourth and ninth steps because they creaked. She avoided Deborah's room and headed for the kitchen. Squishing herself into a corner by the back door, Shannon stared through the breakfast nook windows.

The shadow appeared again. Fluttering between an aspen and an evergreen. An enormous moth that morphed into—

Michael.

Shannon fell back into her corner with a groan.

Why oh *why* was the crazy man creeping around her house at three in the morning?

A less-than-sane part of her yammered accusations that he was the thief.

Her logical side talked her down. Michael knew the security system. He could enter the Paisley mansion anytime— which wouldn't be when she was home.

Yet he was circling her house ... protecting her.

Why? He knew no thief with even one brain cell would return tonight.

So why am I prowling around?

She refused to answer her meddling mind and focused on Michael. Obviously, his obsessive-compulsive police background had gotten the best of him. Or he'd protected her so many times in the past that it had become a bad habit. Or—

Shannon shut down the conjecture. If the phantom haunting her estate grounds had been a burglar, she might have gone after him with the baseball bat. But Michael? She had no desire to confront him.

She finally stopped at the downstairs bathroom and then wearily climbed the marble stairway, almost falling asleep before she reached the top.

— 4 —

What a day.

Shannon tried to concentrate on the bathroom mirror. She aimed a mascara brush at her sandy red lower lashes, but nearly poked herself in the eye.

Great. Smeary brown mascara bruises worked wonders for a girl's appearance. She redid her makeup, wishing she could postpone her date with Hunter. Between the locksmith's comings and goings as he worked on the vault-room, complications in her store's craft classes, and an Elvis-obsessed artist trying to weasel his way into her loft, Shannon hadn't found five minutes to read through her grandfather's logs.

Putting the mascara away, she brushed lint from her indigo pencil skirt and fussed with the scarf she'd beaded to match. Finally, she sank into her bedroom chair. Some days her body felt a hundred years old.

But Hunter's magic often morphed them both into twenty-year-olds again.

Though autumn winds blasted her when she answered the door, his sunlit smile warmed her to her tired toes. "Shannon, you look fantastic."

They shared a sumptuous seafood dinner and a spectacular view of the ocean at a restaurant with a crackling fire and just enough wood smoke. Shannon's muscles unknotted, and she leaned back in her chair with a contented sigh.

"Relaxing?" Hunter, wearing a dark green sweater, khakis, and a great tan, could have modeled for a golf magazine. Even his agate ring matched.

Shannon hugged herself. "I needed this. Time away from the shop. From the house, and all the brouhaha—"

Too late, she clapped a hand to her mouth.

"What happened?" Hunter's forehead puckered.

He'd soon read about it in the newspaper. "Someone broke into the Paisley mansion."

"What?" His strong fingers grasped hers. "When did this happen?"

She shifted her gaze to the roiling waves outside. "The night before last."

His eyes widened. "Why didn't you call me? I would have come right away."

And you would have run into Michael. Trying to squelch that picture, Shannon said, "There was no need. The police came immediately and patrolled the estate during the night. Plus, Deborah loaded her gun, and my mother stayed overnight, cuddling a baseball bat and pepper spray."

Hunter chuckled. "No prowler in his right mind would want to face them."

"They scared me more than the burglar did!" Shannon kept her tone light. *Let's talk about something else ….*

"Did he take anything?"

She shook her head. "Nothing valuable." Shannon wouldn't mention the secret room, not until she understood more about it. "My housekeeper surprised the guy before he could clean us out."

"You could have surprised him." Hunter's hand rose to

caress her face. "I'm so glad you didn't."

Her cheeks warmed at his touch. "So am I."

"Are you sure you don't want me to stay downstairs tonight?" He gently fingered a stray curl of her hair. "I can't bear the thought of anything happening to you."

She pictured explaining the arrangement to Deborah in the morning—although, if Deborah encountered Hunter during the night, she and her gun might not wait for explanations. "I'm not sure that's a good idea."

She couldn't imagine justifying the situation to her twins either.

And what if Michael prowled around the Paisley estate again? Another traitorous flush crept up her face. She closed her eyes.

"Are you OK?" he asked.

"I'm fine. I mean, I'll be fine." She patted his hand. "That's not necessary; I have plenty of protection. But thank you for caring."

"Call me, night or day, if you need me," Hunter insisted.

"I will."

*   *   *

"Let's booby-trap your lawn." Joyce Buchanan's blue eyes glinted as she gouged an invisible intruder with her knitting needles. "If he comes back, that scuzball will regret the day he ever thought of breaking into your house."

"Grayson probably wouldn't like that." Wiping whipped cream from her Espresso Yourself apron, Shannon served Joyce a second hazelnut latte, then gave her a hug. Minefields aside, she thanked God for her loyal friends.

"I assume Michael Stone checked your security system." Betty zoomed through a row of stitches, her fingers a blur.

"He did, and I changed the code, as he suggested." Shannon hesitated, then said, "I talked with him this morning. His forensic tests found nothing."

Nothing was the key word here. Talking to Michael had seemed like talking to a recording. She removed her messy apron, pulled her favorite red chair up to the Purls' knitting circle, and resumed knitting a lavender throw for a nursing home.

Betty's keen gaze probed Shannon. Melanie glanced at her too, but they turned their attention to Kate, who continued bemoaning a troublemaking English Mastiff that had disrupted her obedience classes.

Shannon exhaled. Betty and Melanie knew Michael was a taboo subject at the moment.

Joyce didn't let that bother her. "That guy is crazy about you, Shannon. Surely he can do something more—"

"Which guy do you mean, Joyce?" Kate teased. "Hunter—Michael—or both?"

Shannon ignored them. "The newspaper didn't include everything about the burglary. I wanted to tell you all more about it tonight."

The Purls sat up in unison.

"Please tell me this was just a plain, ordinary burglary," Kate said, putting her knitting aside, her unruly canine pupil forgotten.

"Like that would make it better?" Joyce snorted. "Kate, your instincts are right, though. Something weird is going on." She crossed her arms. "OK, girlfriend, spill it. What's up?"

Shannon took a deep breath. "Well, the burglar found a secret room under the back staircase and took something, but I don't know what."

They stared at Shannon. For a moment, even Joyce fell silent.

"Grandfather Paisley built the room behind a sidewall of a closet under the back stairs, where he kept his stuff. No one in the house knew about it."

Raised eyebrows all around.

Shannon continued, "I skimmed through a decade's worth of paperwork, hoping I could find a contractor's name. Nada. I think Grandfather built it himself."

She told the Purls about the room's contents, the outline in the drawer's dust, and the desk's false back and empty partition.

"Perhaps he hid cash in the compartment. Or important documents," Melanie guessed.

Kate clasped her hands. "Maybe the print in the desk was from a mini treasure chest."

"Beth said Grandfather brought Victoria jewelry after some of his voyages; he brought Beth trinkets too." Shannon clicked her tongue. "Somehow, though, I don't think this involves trinkets."

"So what are you going to do?" As usual, Betty cut to the chase. "And how can we help?"

"I'm so glad you asked." Shannon grinned and nodded toward two big boxes pushed against a coffeehouse wall. "Those are Grandfather's captain's logs. They're full of nautical terms I don't understand, but he also listed everyday events in his life. I want to read them all eventually, but because of the robbery, it's important I find clues he might have dropped—fast. Anything that might help me to understand why he built the secret room and who else knew about it."

Betty's face lit up. "You'd like us to read them for you?"

"I wouldn't ask friends to slog through every line. His handwriting is cramped and hard on the eyes. Rows and rows of numbers and measurements I don't understand." Shannon made a face. "I've hired a retired naval officer to review them. But while he's working on one box, I wondered if you each would take home a book, skim it, and summarize your findings."

Melanie grimaced. "What if we miss something?"

"I could easily miss something too. Until now, Old Blue is the only connection I've had with my grandfather." Shannon bit her lip. "I'm not feeling very objective right now."

"Gee, why not?" Joyce rolled her eyes. "Just because ever since you came to America, creeps have been popping out of the woodwork—"

"Friends too." Shannon looked around at the Purls, her adopted sisters. "Wonderful friends."

"Bring on the books." Betty pulled two of the large, heavy logs from the box.

Kate dragged the box to their knitting nook. "Just think, we get to snoop in somebody's diaries, and we won't get in trouble with our parents."

"I haven't read anything questionable." Shannon paused. "But I never knew my grandfather. I can't make any guarantees."

"So what?" Melanie patted Shannon on the shoulder. "All families have a skeleton or two hidden in their closets."

"I only found a secret room—thank goodness," Shannon half-joked, half-shivered.

Smiling, Melanie patted Shannon on the shoulder. "What you share with the Purls goes into the prayers of the Purls. Nowhere else."

"Hear, hear." Joyce waved her sparkly, half-finished magenta scarf at Shannon. "Remember all the stuff I had to share about my past when Grayson thought I'd killed Old Man Percy with my cupcakes? You used it to help me. We want to be there for you too."

"Of course, you're right." Tears formed in Shannon's eyes again—as they had far too often as of late. "It's just that I've always wanted a granddad. Grandfather looks so big and handsome and brave in his portrait—"

"From what I understand, he was all of those things. My parents thought very highly of Captain Paisley," Betty said.

Who could remain gloomy in the light of her smile?

Shannon lifted her head and picked up her knitting project again. "Thanks. Thanks so much. I don't know what we'll find, but help yourself to anything in the box." She paused. "I need to know the truth."

* * *

"Blue dragon?" Shannon squinted at the faded words penciled on the last page of James's 1957 log, one of his final notes. "'Met with Barnwell. Fought with doc. Hid stowaway in the blue dragon.' What does that mean?"

She set the book beside her bedroom computer and searched the Web. The grandfather clock in the upstairs hallway struck eleven.

Go to bed by one. You have to, Shannon reminded herself.

Even if life had been normal, her full schedule tomorrow would push her past her limits. She should have been asleep an hour ago.

Before long, though, she lost herself in research. *Hmm. No one played video games during the fifties so that can't be the blue dragon in Grandfather's log ... oh, great.* She peered at purply wads of dried plants on her screen. Blue Dragon was also a name for a potent form of marijuana. Shannon closed her eyes, calmed her throbbing heart, and summoned some logic. In 1957, drug trafficking hadn't yet reached epidemic levels. She'd need to see more evidence before she believed her grandfather had been involved in something like that.

Besides, didn't they call it hashish then? Shannon quizzed her tired brain. *I really, really hope that's not what he meant.*

Nevertheless, she made a note to tell the Purls to watch for any drug terms, old or new, in the logs they took home.

Shannon forced her fingers to tap more keys. She found a cargo ship in the United Kingdom called the Blue Dragon, plus a kind of training sailboat. Both currently in use. Could James have hidden something on one of those ships? Her pulse quickened.

He might have listed it elsewhere in his captain's logs. Another sticky note for the Purls.

Even if no one found the Blue Dragon among her grandfather's entries, surely someone kept records of boats that docked in and around Apple Grove. The Coast Guard? The state? She'd check first with the local marina. Tomorrow, if possible—

Chill, Shannon. That was back in 1957. Her initial elation faded. Even if she found a record of a ship called the Blue Dragon, it probably no longer existed. If James had hidden something there, the chances of finding it ranged from remote to zero.

Listlessly, she scanned several more screens. A delicate, palm-size blue-gray sea creature appeared, looking as if it had flown out of a Pokémon cartoon. So "blue dragon" also referred to this pretty but poisonous sea slug from the coasts of South Africa and Australia. Plus a Chinese holiday, a tea set, sports teams, and a number of restaurants and spas.

Enough. Shannon clasped her hands around her aching neck. She needed a break. She slipped downstairs, having warned Deborah of her night wanderings before she retired.

"I'm glad you locked up all those ships and things at Michael's," her housekeeper had said, "and that you've divvied up most of Captain Paisley's logs. If that burglar comes back, he won't find anything to steal—other than your grandmother's art and antiques."

Shannon wished the thief could see Deborah's dangerous smile as she loaded her gun. It had become a nightly ceremony.

Passing the dining room with its elegant portraits and silver, Shannon considered why she didn't worry more about her household valuables.

Somehow, she knew. Deep inside, she understood that the thief was after something else. But what?

This isn't 'taking a break.' Shannon shushed her questions and heated hot chocolate in her favorite butterfly mug. Her thoughts wandered to semester's end, when she and Old Blue would chug to Portland, pick up her twins, and bring them home.

How Lara hated to be seen in Shannon's old truck.

The "evil mother" smile she usually hid from her children surfaced, full and satisfying. If her sophisticated daughter wanted to come home, she'd ride in Old Blue, even if she said it spewed smoke like a nauseous dragon....

Dragon.

Blue dragon.

Shannon gurgled her hot chocolate.

Could it be?

She stuck her mug in the fridge, grabbed a coat and stocking cap she wore for yard work, and charged into the night with Deborah's flashlight. The ivy-covered garage, once the mansion's carriage house, loomed nearby.

The security lights spotlighted her like a performer onstage. Shannon dashed to the garage, knowing that if Mr. Creep had returned, he'd already seen her. Tapping a code into the venerable garage's keypad always made her feel anachronistic, but she gave silent thanks for the security system as she slipped inside and flicked on lights. Shadows lurked, clutching at her with ghostly hands, but she ignored them.

She opened Old Blue's front passenger door and shined the flashlight into the glove compartment. She poked a hand under the seat, behind the seat. She yanked out floor mats. Nothing.

Shannon ran the flashlight under the truck's wide fenders and heavy chrome bumpers. She opened the truck's hood and stared at the maze of motor parts until her eyes watered. With a grunt, she pulled a car dolly from its hooks on the wall, lay on it, and rolled herself under Old Blue.

Just what do you think you're going to see, Shannon? You don't know a carburetor from a transmission.

She had to look. She just had to.

Despite the flashlight's comforting beam, the truck's grimy blackness closed in on her. Pipes and parts writhed in dark labyrinths. What if the chassis, exhausted after more than a half century, dropped on her? Who would hear her scream, even if she had breath to yell?

She couldn't make her arms and legs move as her claustrophobia set in. How she edged herself out from under Old Blue, she would never remember. But she finally rose from the dolly and stumbled from the garage back to the mansion.

Maybe you overreacted just a little? Shannon wished, for the thousandth time, that close spaces didn't affect her so much. Entering the foyer, she glanced at a mirror and saw that grease dotted and striped her favorite PJs, her hands, and her face. The German cuckoo clock in her study chirped the hour.

A bath at 2:30 a.m.?

Though exhausted, she made herself scrub away the grime, then fell into bed, hoping for a few hours of sleep.

But she'd left her mind in the garage, probing, poking, trying to see what wasn't there.

Was she way off base? Even if James's cryptic words did point to his favorite truck, that didn't necessarily connect them to the tiny vault-room.

Or had he placed a key clue in Old Blue after all?

Shannon finally dozed off, still debating. She spent the remainder of the night swimming through big breakers with lovely but deadly blue Pokémon sea slugs.

5

"**W**hat were you thinking, messing around under that old truck in the middle of the night?" Deborah stuck her dishwater-soapy hands on her hips. "Out in that dark garage, alone. You could have run into you-know-who."

Shannon sighed as she packed her lunch. "You're right. I wasn't thinking. I wanted to know if Grandfather left something important in Old Blue."

"Then take it to a mechanic. Just because Captain Paisley did all his maintenance himself doesn't mean you know what you're doing." Deborah thumped the copper teakettle back onto the kitchen range.

Shannon's mind was already running along that thread. She called a garage, stuffed her lunch and work materials into her briefcase, and chugged to town.

"Man, she's a beauty." The mechanic's eyes shone with as much admiration as if Old Blue were a Miss Oregon.

Guys. Shannon grinned wearily and shoved her keys across the counter. "It probably needs an overall checkup. Please look it over very carefully. Call me if you find *anything* unusual. Anything."

He blinked. "OK. You need a ride somewhere?"

"No, walking to work will wake me up." She needed a jump start today.

Fall mornings in Apple Grove often meant fog and

drizzle, but today the weather seemed to understand that Shannon needed sunlight more than a double espresso. A mild breeze off the ocean tickled her cheeks as she walked. Pots of purple and yellow chrysanthemums hung from the old-fashioned lampposts, brightening the downtown's fresh-scrubbed face.

As she walked, though, Shannon's mood unraveled like a row of flawed stitches. She peered into the alleys she passed and cast several glances behind her.

She saw only townspeople, who smiled greetings at her.

Oh, no. Not that somebody's-following-me feeling again. Deborah was right. Late nights and sessions with Old Blue in the spooky garage did nothing to balance her equilibrium. Tonight, Shannon decided, she would go to bed by nine.

Blackness halted her in her tracks. Big, hot hands clapped over her eyes. She heard a scream that terrified her even more. Then she realized it erupted from her own throat.

"Shannon, I'm sorry! It's just me." Hunter's contrite voice splashed relief and fury through her. His hand rubbed her arm gently, as if calming a fearful child.

"I—I—"

"Are you aware this lady just experienced a break-in?" An angry male voice rumbled from her other side. "You scared her to death."

Michael glowered at Hunter like a ninja warrior. Passersby stopped to stare.

"It's all right, Michael." Flames crept up her cold face.

"I should have thought before I acted. I only meant to tease you, but I can see that was a big mistake." Hunter apologized, but his concerned face hardened. He shot Michael an equally nasty look before he slipped an arm around her. "I'm sorry, Shannon. That was completely crass of me."

Shannon made herself smile. "I'm entirely too jumpy these days."

"Let me make it up to you with a special day." Hunter's eyes softened to the puppy expression that melted her. "Portland. Seattle, if you'd like."

Michael's, however, glowed like molten steel in his rigid face.

"That's not necessary. We're making far too much of this." Shannon gave them each another smile and glanced at her watch. "Essie's probably wondering where I am." She really didn't want to explain to her efficient but occasionally nosy manager why she was late. "I'd better go."

She picked up the briefcase she'd dropped and walked toward the corner.

"I'll call you." Hunter's voice, unnecessarily loud, floated over her shoulder.

Shannon nodded, but she didn't dare look back.

Well, that was juvenile of Hunter. Even more surprising because it was his thoughtfulness that had attracted her from the beginning. But she'd already forgiven him, and he certainly would make it up to her.

A mean little part of her didn't mind that Michael knew that too.

*   *   *

"Weirdest thing I've seen in awhile." The mechanic's down-home accent crackled through Shannon's phone. "Little iron box hid in a hole in your truck's frame."

A current of joy flashed through her as she leaned against her shop's beading counter. *I was right!* She tried to plane excitement from her voice. "Thanks for calling me. Does it have a lock?"

"Yes, ma'am. Looks pretty rusty, though. The box was held in place by magnets, mostly. I woulda missed it if I hadn't gone over it with a fine-toothed comb."

"If you'll keep it in your office, I'll be right there." Shannon hung up.

"What a smile! Did you discover gold?" Essie, fine brows raised over her round brown eyes, hovered near her elbow. "Or did Hunter propose?"

"You and your imagination." Shannon rolled her eyes at her romantic twenty-something assistant, though heat already streamed to her cheeks. "The mechanic says my truck's done. Would you cover for a few minutes, please?"

"Sure." Essie sounded disappointed and a little suspicious.

Shannon grabbed her coat and left. The supposed proposal by Hunter was, of course, pure nonsense.

But was Essie right about the gold?

*   *   *

"Here y'are." The mechanic handed her the rusty, heavy little box. His eyes, enfolded in smile wrinkles, gleamed. "Was your grandpa some kind of FBI agent?"

Though Shannon's heart thumped like a tom-tom, she shrugged. "He was eccentric—just liked hiding things, I guess." If she treated this casually, perhaps this man would too. She wanted to ask him to remove the lock, but if he saw its contents, most of Apple Grove also would know them by evening. "Thanks for your help."

Shannon paid him and slid the box into a shopping bag, itching to know its contents. But no afternoon break materialized. Her customers all needed extra help. The silversmith and beading classes she loved teaching seemed eternal. Finally, after supper, she sequestered herself in her bedroom with the box and her silversmith tools. She set the box on newspapers and poked the lock, probing and wiggling it as rust flaked away.

Clink.

Thud.

Easy. She should have tried to open the box earlier. But privacy didn't exist at her store. And the fewer people who knew about her grandfather's "stowaway," the better. Shannon jiggled the corroded latch, blood pounding in her temples.

The box opened.

A plain, dark blue book, much smaller and thicker than her grandfather's logs. Several hundred pages, at least.

Disappointment slowed her pulse. More stuff to read?

For a moment, Shannon laughed at herself. What had she expected? A gleaming cache of golden coins? A crown to set on her head? Despite the fairy-tale events that had shaped her life recently, she shouldn't expect pirate treasures and poofs of pink smoke every day.

Shannon wedged a fingernail between the first yellowed pages. A journal. What was so special, so different about it? Turning the pages carefully, she skimmed a few entries. Her grandfather's cramped writing, often smeared and hard to read. That was the same. But this book contained no latitudes or longitudes. No rows of hieroglyphic readings. Instead, sporadic entries, often a year or more apart, chronicled his searching for something. Well, she'd never know unless she read it. Surely his accounts would steer her in the right direction.

Shannon curled up in her comfy bedroom chair, covering herself with Grandmother Victoria's colorful butterfly afghan as she turned back to the opening entries of Grandfather James's journal, dated 1942.

Between voyages, James and someone named Corny scoured an undeveloped area near Apple Grove, seeking a treasure.

A treasure.

Shannon closed her eyes. She again savored the gleam of gold she'd wanted to find hidden in Old Blue, the fantasy of glittering jeweled necklaces and rings.

Perhaps her fairy-tale imaginings might prove real.

Shannon returned to the journal, inhaling pages like oxygen, only to discover James and Corny had labored endlessly with no results.

See? You let yourself get carried away.

Grandfather had too. What kept him pushing, digging, searching?

From the pages of the journal, he answered her. Despite his father's opposition, James's granddad had fed him stories about their ancestor's treasure since he was a child. "Dinna forget your canny fore-elder Angus Paisley, a sailor who made away with a bonnie bit o' Captain Drake's treasure, richt under his nose!"

Drake? Sir Francis Drake? Or some unknown, unlucky sea captain swindled by Grandfather's ancestor?

Her ancestor too, she realized.

Or did her "fore-elder" require only his just desserts? Perhaps his captain had cheated him and refused him the fair share he had earned.

She hugged Victoria's afghan. When Shannon came to America seeking family, she had not grasped the complications involved. Some of her new relatives, to her dismay, had proven deceptive and greedy. Now, among her ancestors, would she find even more crooked branches she'd just as soon lop off her family tree?

She returned to the journal text itself. It gave more information about the legendary Angus, handed down by Paisleys through the centuries. It seems her "canny" ancestor, the disgraced son of a clan chief, became a sailor who worked on Sir Francis Drake's ships. Drake raided Spanish galleons returning from the Far East, but storms blew his ship off course. When it landed on the Oregon Coast, Angus hid a portion of his captain's treasure there. He planned to return someday for his loot. A lover of riddles, he concocted his map using clues rather than navigational numbers, listing them on the back.

Shannon supposed his scheme made sense, especially if he were trying to hide the location from his enemies— and perhaps his friends, if they were like him! But Angus died before he could reclaim his treasure. He handed down the map to his sons, sans solutions, saying he'd used his brains—and they could too.

Nice dad. Shannon waded through James's endless entries about tramping through thorny underbrush and poking around rocks. Two years of hard work, with nothing to show for it. Several accounts described how James and Corny, after fruitless searches, drowned their disappointment at favorite taverns.

Shannon's grandmother, not surprisingly, had reproached James for his frequent absences, especially when he came home drunk at dawn.

> *Victoria doesn't believe me when I tell her I've only been treasure-hunting. I suppose I've given her reason to imagine the worst ….*

Victoria, who had made Shannon her heir, obviously resented her husband's treasure hunt. Shannon winced. *Are you looking over my shoulder, Grandmother?*

Several paragraphs later, Shannon found her mother's name.

> *Beth is young, but already, like Victoria, she wants nothing to do with the treasure. Both think my brain is pickled in salt brine.*

Shannon put down the journal in a daze. *Beth knows about the treasure.*

Beth had dashed to Shannon's side after the burglary, seen the secret room, armed her with a bat and pepper spray, and said not one word about James's treasure quest.

Obviously, her mother still followed Victoria's lead.

No wonder Beth had seemed shell-shocked that evening. And less than enthusiastic about Shannon's desire to know James.

The grandfather clock in the hallway struck two doleful gongs that sounded as weary as she felt. Commanding her eyelids to stay open, she made herself read another account of a midnight search of a beach area Grandfather called Parable Rock. She'd never heard of it, but that didn't surprise her, having lived in Apple Grove only a couple years. Maybe Deborah knew about Parable Rock.

And out of the blue, some odd reference to a "dark glass." Shannon hadn't a clue.

Her eyes rebelled anew, and Shannon sank into stupor … until the word "doubloon" burned into her gaze.

We found the gold doubloon Angus buried. At last.

Her grandfather described the tarnished coin with its barely legible cross and lion on its coat of arms. Any fatigue disappeared—like a poof of pink smoke. Shannon skimmed the lines. Surely the coin didn't comprise the entire treasure. Would her grandfather have searched so diligently for one old coin, valuable though it might be?

No, he regarded it as an indication the treasure was real. That he was on the right track, and it was located somewhere nearby. She didn't know why. But she would find out.

The question that had swum under the surface all evening leaped like a dolphin: *Did Grandfather ever find the treasure?*

She had to know the end of the story. Shannon quickly but gently turned fragile pages to the final entry.

October 5, 1957.
I know the treasure is not a figment of my imagination, nor the product of my dreams when I was younger.

I've spent much of my life so far searching for the treasure. Yet God has denied me what I wanted most. He is smarter than I gave Him credit for. Father said Christ gives mercy to prodigals and fools. I pray he's right.

I must keep the map safe for Beth. Perhaps someday, her sharp little mind may deduce what I haven't yet, and the treasure will secure her future. Maybe she will realize that despite my faults, I truly loved her.

Shannon blinked to keep tears from dropping onto the book. The writing blurred as she turned the page.

But not so much that she couldn't see the crude map.

— 6 —

Shannon's fingers trembled as she tried to follow the messy penciled lines of what appeared to be a shoreline. A few squiggles, humps, and smeary dots. No words, only initials. No numbers or measurements. And no "X marks the spot." If this was the map Grandfather mentioned earlier, no wonder he and his granddad hadn't found the treasure.

Shannon chided herself. Of course, this couldn't be *the* map, the one Angus had drawn centuries before ....

An idea whispered in her mind. Her skin prickled.

The thief who broke into her house had been searching for something in the secret room.

The map and the gold doubloon.

Shannon was sure of it.

She inspected the drawing again. James must have sketched a copy in his journal. Thank heaven. Otherwise, how could she even begin to solve the mysteries that suddenly shrouded her days?

However, Grandfather drew it for his own convenience, not for that of a granddaughter he never knew. He understood what the letters and scratchings meant.

Shannon didn't.

After scouring the map again, she turned the page. A few smudged words in a list. She squinted at the first one. "S-i—"

She couldn't decipher the next letters, so she took a

magnifying glass from her desk drawer, one she used when fine beadwork strained her eyes. S-i-m-m-u-e-m.

Simmuem.

Shannon scrambled to her computer and searched. Though still unfamiliar with some of Oregon's geography, she'd been right! The Simmuem River flowed from the Cascades to the Pacific, only fifteen or twenty miles away. A unique name—possibly Native American?—that probably wouldn't be duplicated elsewhere. On the map, a faded line curlicued inland from the coastline. Sure enough, James had labeled it "S." So this short list reflected Angus's clues, the ones he'd written on the back of his map?

Shannon slowly decoded more words, occasionally using the magnifying glass. *Grandfather, you certainly didn't make this easy.*

Sidhe Glen—Graves
Black Donald's Hand
Parable Rock

Parable Rock. Of course. Shannon wanted to dance a Highland Fling. James and Corny found the doubloon at Parable Rock! She located "PR" on her grandfather's sketch, near the ocean.

Her elation soon leveled off when she combed maps online for the name. Nothing. Shannon shifted her analysis back to Sidhe Glen.

"Yesss!"

That location didn't appear on the maps either, but a cemetery and a Native American burial ground were located inland, south of the Simmuem.

Impulsively, Shannon half-rose from her desk, but outside the windows, the sleet-filled night wind howled its protest. Its clamor, however, couldn't compete with the chorus of outrage she'd hear from her friends if they discovered she'd been poking around graveyards alone at night. Not that they'd jump at the chance to join her.

Actually, Shannon didn't relish the prospect either, especially after the burglary. She sat again and carved out space in her daytime schedule to explore them ASAP.

First she should find out if the graveyards even existed during Angus's era. Shannon tapped the keys, confirming her suspicions. Few Europeans landed on the Oregon shores in the late sixteenth century, let alone lived long enough in the area to die there. The Native American burial ground might prove a better possibility.

Shannon continued her research of the other words James had listed. She drew an imaginary line from Sidhe Glen—"SG" on James's map—straight south to "BDH," Black Donald's Hand. For centuries, "Black Donald" had appeared in Scottish folklore as another name for the devil. Again, no such address on contemporary maps. According to her grandfather, though, Parable Rock was located directly west of Black Donald's Hand, whatever that was. Perhaps a rock formation?

Shannon shifted her attention to the list. Two more clues to consider.

Witch Cave.

First, burial grounds and landmarks named after the devil, and now Witch Cave. Shannon frowned. She certainly couldn't nominate this ancestor for sainthood. She did the now-familiar coastline search on the Web and struck out again. She summoned James's map. No "WC" anywhere, though he'd labeled a coastal spot "WWW." Probably didn't stand for "World Wide Web."

No "DG" for "dark glass," either, the generic last clue on the list.

By now, Shannon's brain didn't know its left side from its right. She'd pursue the mystery tomorrow.

She sipped stone-cold tea and tried not to think about the burglary, but questions nibbled, then gnawed at her.

How did the burglar know where to find the map? How had he learned about the treasure?

Certainly not from her. She hadn't even known the secret room existed, let alone a hidden cache of ... what?

Who else knew about the treasure? James's accomplice certainly did—he called him Corny, didn't he? She'd check that out. He told Victoria and Beth too. *Did Grandfather tell anyone else?*

Did the burglar know about the journal? Perhaps he simply couldn't find it.

And perhaps he was watching her, hoping she would lead him to it.

Shannon's blood ran cold. She'd convinced herself that her uneasiness downtown was caused by Hunter sneaking up on her and Michael's uncanny way of materializing when she was afraid. Such a ridiculous scene. Remembering their faces, she tried to eke out a chuckle.

But her instincts insisted she'd been followed by someone else.

Someone up to no good.

Shudders climbed up her spine like sharp-clawed cats.

Should she tell Michael about the journal?

Her annoying intuition demanded she should. Shannon crossed her arms. "If I do, then I'll hire him as a professional. No more buddy-buddy stuff."

She didn't want to think about Michael either. Definitely time for bed.

But the journal met her eye. Where could she hide it overnight? She didn't fully trust the security system, nor the vault-room lock.

Shannon rose, journal in hand. Weaving as she crossed the room, she steadied herself and checked for the baseball bat and pepper spray. Shannon climbed up the stepstool she'd finally purchased, then fell onto the big bed. She stuffed the journal inside the bottom pillow, squished the second pillow on top, and plopped into their softness, praying for a quiet, boring night.

*　　*　　*

"Haven't you dealt with enough? I'd hoped you could bypass that whole treasure thing." Beth had brightened at Shannon's arrival for an afternoon break at Joyce's bakery, Pink Sprinkles. Now her mother slumped in the shiny black booth.

"The secret room, the burglary, Grandfather's journal—they all fell into my lap. I didn't intend to become a treasure hunter."

Shannon wished they could stick to gabbing about the twins and her latest date with Hunter while devouring Joyce's yummy cupcakes. But the sooner Shannon dealt with the crazy treasure business, the more likely she would discover the thief.

That was her theory, and for now, she was sticking to it.

Shannon cleared her throat. "Do you have any idea what kind of treasure Grandfather was seeking? Gold doubloons? Lottery tickets?"

Beth laughed, but her green eyes faded to gray. "Gold, certainly. Sir Francis Drake—"

"So Angus did steal the treasure from Drake." Shannon tried to silence the excitement in her voice.

Beth shrugged. "That's the story Father told."

"You think he embroidered a little?"

That sterile laugh again. "Father could invent yarns with the best of them. He tried to convince Mother the treasure included a huge pearl, unmatched in all the Orient."

Shannon fidgeted with her tea. *Perhaps Grandfather and his granddad—and how many other Paisleys down through the years?—possessed overly active imaginations.*

But how many burglars would embrace such a risk for imaginary treasure?

Shannon said lightly, "Well, my unwelcome guest seems to have taken Grandfather's tale seriously."

Beth threw her a sharp look. "You think he was looking for the treasure?"

"I think he took the original map and the gold doubloon Grandfather describes in his journal." Shannon fingered a stubborn curl away from her face. "What puzzles me is why he hid the journal in Old Blue, rather than in the secret room, along with the map and doubloon. It's almost as if he expected a rival to seek the treasure, so he concealed pieces of the puzzle in different places."

"Where's the journal now?"

Shannon glanced around the empty bakery. The shop's shades, drawn to shield them from afternoon sun, also protected them from prying eyes. Slowly Shannon slipped the fat little book from an inner coat pocket and passed it to her mother.

Beth's eyes widened as if she held dynamite.

"I've been keeping it in my lockbox at the bank, but I wanted you to see it." Shannon realized she was whispering. "Aren't you going to open it?"

Beth hesitated, then edged a pink fingernail under the cover. Slowly, she leafed through several entries. "It's Father's handwriting, all right. I sometimes sneaked into his library and played with the things on his desk, tried to read his letters—anything to feel closer to him."

"Do you remember seeing this book?" Shannon tried to curb her eagerness.

"I may have seen Father writing in it a time or two." A wan smile curled Beth's lips. "Whenever I did, he kicked me out of the library." Her free hand gently stroked the journal's back, but she made no effort to read further. "This treasure may not even exist, yet it consumed Father all his life. It caused my mother and me endless grief."

Shannon caught her breath at the icy flame in Beth's eyes.

Her mother shut the small book, her fingers white-knuckled around it. "Shannon, it would be best if you forgot you ever saw this."

*   *   *

Shannon almost wished Michael had forgotten to show up at Fairmont Beach, their proposed meeting spot, away from Apple Grove's curious eyes. But there he stood, solid and immovable as the rocks around him, the ocean and sky a brilliant blue backdrop for Mr. America.

She welcomed Michael's strength—on this surprisingly lovely day, the thin jacket he wore couldn't hide his muscles—and she welcomed his investigator's savvy, so valuable in solving past problems.

If only she didn't have to ask for his help again. A small pool of irritation simmered inside Shannon. *Just remember, Mister, I'm paying your full fee. You work for me.*

He gestured at ocean waves licking at their feet. "We'd better hurry. The tide's rolling in."

"I'll be brief."

As they walked in the fresh, salty air, she told him about searching for the journal in Old Blue. His right eyebrow rose. When his lips flattened to a straight line, she fought to keep from grinning.

In anyone else, these reactions meant little. But on Michael's face—

"Why didn't you call me?" he demanded.

"I generally don't call people in the middle of the night. Especially when there is no immediate danger." Shannon kept her voice measured. "Besides, I did hire you, once I read about the treasure map—"

"Treasure map?"

"Yes. My ancestor Angus Paisley drew it and passed it down in our family. I think the burglar stole it from my grandfather's secret room, along with an old Spanish doubloon."

The more she told him, the faster he walked.

"Would you please slow down?" She hadn't dressed for a race.

He did—for four steps. "I knew I shouldn't let you stay in that house."

Shannon stopped and stabbed her hips with her hands. "I'm perfectly capable of taking care of myself, thank you very much." *Especially with Deborah and her gun downstairs.*

Michael glared at her. "If the burglar hasn't yet found the treasure, he'll watch you, thinking he'll learn more. If he hears you've discovered your grandfather's journal, he might strike again—"

"I know. That's why I hired you." *Although we might kill each other before somebody else does.* Shannon bent, picked up a slippery rock, and let it fly, splitting a white-plumed wave. She flung another.

"My first recommendation is that you stay elsewhere for awhile. Maybe at Betty's inn."

She pictured sleeping in a lovely room at the friendly, well-populated Apple Grove Inn downtown. Quite a contrast to another scary night in the big bed in the big, empty mansion out in the country—

No. Shannon raised her chin. *I won't let this burglar creep chase me out of my own house.* Aloud, she coated her words with civility. "I don't think so."

Michael groaned. "I wish you'd at least argue with me. When you use that tone—"

She pumped in more syrup. "What tone?"

"That sticky-sweet tone that says you won't budge an inch." He jammed his hands into his pockets. After a moment, he said, "If you insist on staying in that old mausoleum, make sure you're never alone. Especially at night."

Certainly, Michael was right about that. If Deborah needed to visit her elderly relatives, Shannon might stay with one of the Purls. "What's your next recommendation?"

"I assume you won't copy the journal and lend it to me …."

You assume right. She wanted to be the first to read her grandfather's personal account cover to cover. Maybe later—

"Keep me updated on what you find out," Michael growled. "At least once daily. Better yet, check in twice a day. I have a bad feeling about this burglar." He frowned. "You should buy a firearm and learn to use it."

"You and Deborah." Shannon rolled her eyes.

"I'm serious. You attract more trouble than a dog does fleas."

Thank you for that flattering analogy. Shannon counted to ten before she answered. "I will check in with you regularly. Twice a day, even. But buy a gun? I'll have to think about that." She brushed the thought aside, not wanting to admit, even to herself, that real danger lurked. She hurried to change the subject. "I wanted to tell you about the Corny guy Grandfather mentions in his journal."

"Corny?" Michael's eyebrows shot up again.

"Yes. His full name, according to Deborah, was Cornelius Hansen. He was a sailor who helped James look for the treasure. Corny was younger than Grandfather; I hoped I might find him alive, or his family. But Deborah said he died during World War II." Shannon sighed. "I checked the records and confirmed it. He was only in his late teens, single, and without family, as far as I can tell. Grandfather mentions he was drafted and missed his help, but that's all, so far. So I've hit a dead end."

Michael seemed to be half-listening. Stuck in his "recommendations" rut.

Shannon counted to fifteen. "All right, what else do you think I should do?"

To her surprise, he hesitated.

"Surely, you have more advice for me," she pressed.

Those oh-so-blue eyes pierced hers. "I don't think you'll like this recommendation."

"Tell me anyway."

"I've rechecked the backgrounds of the people you deal with."

You're right. I don't like this. But it makes sense. She narrowed her eyes. "Any problems?"

"Beware of that extra-friendly ceramics whiz who wants to rent space in your loft." He smiled mirthlessly. "She writes checks on nothing and disappears overnight."

"I'd already sensed red flags." Having run the business a few years, she'd learned to spot losers. But why was Michael looking at her like that?

"I also ran a more in-depth background check on Hunter Banks."

Not this again. Anger crashed through her, strangling the words that tried to form in her throat. "You've already told me the business he works for doesn't exist—and you're wrong about that. Bayside Marine Research Associates does exist. It's new."

"We'll have to agree to disagree about that." Michael paused. "There's more."

Shannon crossed her arms. "What?"

"He's not exactly what he seems. He's an adjunct professor in marine biology at Lawson College, outside Eureka, California. He did win a grant to do research along the Oregon Coast." Michael paused. "But that grant would never support him for this long. He's stayed in Apple Grove for months—and I'm sure you're aware he isn't pinching pennies."

Shannon chiseled her words. "Did you ever think he might have drawn support from elsewhere—like the business he's affiliated with? Or maybe he's saved for years so he could complete his work? Or perhaps he received an inheritance."

Michael raised his chin and his voice. "I've checked into every possibility. At least, every legitimate one."

So who are you, Inspector Infallible? "*Every* possibility?" she blurted. "Including the chance you may not be quite as objective as you think?"

His eyes hardened into gray-blue granite. He said nothing.

She wanted to push him and his presumptuous attitude off the barnacle-encrusted rocks and watch huge, hungry tongues of water carry him out to sea.

Instead, she whipped around and stomped toward the parking lot.

Grandfather, you and I may find this treasure by ourselves.

— 7 —

The November wind tried to slap some sense into Shannon. *You left work early for this?*

She wore clam-digging boots, so her toes stayed dry as she clumped along the beach—dry, but stiff with cold. Winds off the sullen ocean penetrated her parka.

Weather or no weather, she couldn't stay away from Smugglers' Cove, James's undocumented name for the area around the Simmuem River. *Not sure I want to know why he called it that.*

Certainly, the dark implications fit the landscape today. Wraithlike mists hovered over the gray Simmuem and its footbridge. They taunted the brooding, green-black hills facing the beach. According to Grandfather's journal, Black Donald's Hand could be seen from the beach. Though located an unknown distance inland, it was in a direct line with Parable Rock on the shoreline.

Not a good day to look for the Hand, perhaps, but she had to grab an hour or two when she could.

She'd called Michael, who also questioned her timing—not only because of the storm warnings, but because he couldn't come with her.

She wouldn't miss him.

She couldn't wait one minute longer to explore her journal findings.

So she walked.

And walked.

One mile. Perhaps two, combing the hillsides for fingers of jutting rock. She cast an occasional glance over her shoulder and reached inside her parka pocket to touch Beth's can of pepper spray. But she encountered only one fanatical jogger on the lonely beach.

Nothing pointed to Black Donald's Hand. Not surprising, as dozens of mist-wraiths now drifted in a melancholy dance across ridges and canyons.

Wearily, she turned around. She'd kept her eyes peeled for the Hand on the way. Shannon decided that on the way back, she would explore the rocks along the beach. But the tide already lapped closer; she'd have to hurry. She stepped gingerly onto the first group of pillow-shaped black boulders, slippery, as if greased. Lots of tidal pools dotted with anemones.

She climbed the next group of rocks. And the next.

Though her brain often forgot where she'd put her keys, it somehow remembered her college geology class, and she was able to identify primary components of the terrain. Basalt. Scoria.

But Shannon saw nothing to point her to Parable Rock.

"Why couldn't Angus just post a sign?" she muttered.

Despite Angus's background, the rock's name seemed to point to Christ's parable about the lost coin. Though a sixteenth-century pirate might spurn Christianity, his culture probably influenced him.

How would such a clue help her identify the rock where James found the doubloon? What personal significance did Angus attach to it? What shape reflected the word *parable*?

If I stumbled onto it, I might walk right by.

Even if she discovered the location, where was Witch

Cave? Numerous little caverns honeycombed the rocks and hills. Because of the discrepancy in the initials, she couldn't assume it was located at the point James had marked WWW. Even if she could, neither map nor clue pinpointed to that spot, distance-wise. No reference to a landmark that would tell her, either. All she knew was that "WWW" was located "nearby," south of Parable Rock.

She had to try. Shannon climbed more rocks. An extra-large wave slopped briny water into her boots and nearly threw her off her perch. Spreading her arms like a tightrope walker, Shannon made her way back to the sand. Her boots weighed a ton apiece as she plodded along the shore.

The blue-purple clouds on the horizon didn't bode well. Neither did the snuffly feeling expanding in her nose and chest.

Grandfather must have felt this way a thousand times. She marveled at his fortitude, even if motivated by greed.

A pirate-tale treasure intrigued her. But unlike James, she didn't want its wealth.

She only wanted peace in her life again.

And if finding Angus's booty would help accomplish that, like her grandfather, she would not give up.

*　　　*　　　*

"Mum, what's this about a burglary?" Alec's no-nonsense tone, so like his father's, jolted Shannon from her store inventory with Essie.

"Why didn't you tell us?" Lara's voice rose like the upper register of a pipe organ.

Great. Shannon gulped. Why were conference calls

invented, anyway? Now both twins could gang up on her. "Ah ... just a minute, OK?"

She gestured to Essie, who resumed her review of the thousands of beads on display. Shannon dashed to her office, phone to her ear. "I meant to call you both, but things have been crazy—"

"So we heard."

Shannon didn't have to imagine Alec's glowering, freckled face. "I suppose Chief Grayson contacted you."

"Yes, and he's questioning our friends." Lara squealed with indignation. "Mum, you know how I hated that when Mr. Percy died. Why didn't you warn us?"

The twins were right, of course. How could she have assumed Grayson wouldn't follow up on his hunches, misguided though they seemed? Shannon bit her lip. "I'm so, so sorry I didn't tell you about the break-in. I didn't want to upset you."

"You think hearing this secondhand doesn't upset us?" Alec growled.

"I do apologize." Shannon dropped into her desk chair and propped her already-pounding forehead with her hand. "Lately, I haven't been thinking clearly."

Silence. Then Lara said, "Mum, are you all right?"

The forlorn question reminded Shannon of days she'd spent on the sofa with the flu, two red-haired toddlers hovering anxiously around her. "I'm fine." She forced herself to smile. "I'm even enjoying the mystery involved in all this—"

"You would."

Shannon couldn't see Alec shake his head, but she knew the gesture all too well. "Come now, don't deny your old mother a little excitement."

"As if you need more." Probably an eye roll from Lara.

Doodling nervously on her phone message pad, Shannon hastened to tell them a limited version of the break-in, including the secret room and its nautical artifacts. She didn't mention the map, journal, or treasure.

"Wow."

Already, Alec's silent questions drained the anger from his voice. Shannon jumped on his curiosity. "A real puzzle, right?"

"Is Michael helping you with this?" Lara still sounded fearful.

"He examined the room." Not that Shannon would welcome Michael's recommendations anytime soon. She jabbed her pen into the pad.

"I'm so glad." Relief flooded Lara's words.

"Me too." Alec echoed her gratitude. "Michael knows what he's doing."

They assumed Michael was working closely with her. A twinge of guilt poked Shannon, but she quieted her fussy conscience by focusing on the break-in. "We all know Chief Grayson leaves no stone unturned. Well, he asked if any of your friends knew our security code."

She could almost hear the twins fidget in unison.

"I told Chaz when we were dating last summer," Lara confessed. "But he would never—"

"I know he wouldn't." Shannon clicked her tongue. "But Grayson—"

"I gave our code to Robert when he had to leave early to go back to Portland," Alec admitted. "To Marcy too. But whether they know the code or not doesn't matter. We, um ...."

Shannon's mother instincts lit up. "You, um, what?"

A pause. "Ah, Mum, we all went skiing in the mountains

the day of the break-in—"

"Instead of going to class?"

"We'd been studying so hard." Lara, a theater major, had always used her talents to wear her parents down. "We needed a little R & R."

"You couldn't ski on a weekend?" A motherly edge crept into Shannon's voice, despite herself.

"The slopes are less crowded during the week and much cheaper," Lara added.

"Safer too." Alec sounded absolutely virtuous. "Anyway— to return to the original point—a bunch of us were skiing that day. The lodge people are confirming it, and eventually Grayson will have to admit we couldn't have been involved. At least, not directly."

"He considers you and Lara suspects?" Now Shannon's voice squeaked like Lara's.

"Of course. You know Grayson."

Oh, yes.

"He's been toughest on Chris," Alec continued. "He was too sick to go skiing that day. Chris even went to the student health center, but Grayson keeps bugging him about his whereabouts."

Remembering the nerdy kid with the taped glasses, Shannon's fists clenched. The police chief had jumped on the fact that Chris was poor. "Tell Chris I don't suspect him and to call me if Grayson leans on him too much."

"Wooo, Grayson had better look out," Alec teased.

"Yeah, he should know better than to mess with our mum." At Lara's cackle, Shannon's tense muscles relaxed.

They laughed and talked a few more minutes, and

Shannon promised to be careful. Thank goodness, the twins accepted her explanations and forgave her.

Hopefully, she'd discover the burglar's identity before she had to tell them more.

*   *   *

Grayson barged through the Paisley Craft Store's door, jangling its bell. He strode to the sewing department in the back of the store, where Shannon was poised on a ladder. "How well do you know Chris Sutton?"

Shannon blinked. *Hello to you too.* She finished clipping a Nativity wall hanging to a ceiling hook and said, "Chris is a friend of the twins. He stayed at our house twice last summer. Why?"

"Hospitality isn't always the best policy." Grayson pushed back strands of his sparse hair. "I think Sutton may be connected with your break-in."

She'd never towered over the police chief before, and she rather liked it. However, she probably should try to settle this face-to-face. Shannon backed down the ladder, turned to the man and said quietly, "Would you mind telling me why you suspect him?"

"You know I can't give out information like that."

"Even to the victim?" She was trying not to cross her arms. Really.

The chief gestured impatiently. "OK. He told us he was too sick to skip class with your kids—claims he went to the student health center. His professor told me Sutton called him that day. Said he couldn't take an exam. But I discovered the kid never went to the health center. Instead, he talked some nurse into a prescription without seeing the doctor."

Chris didn't go to the doctor? Until now, the twins' story had matched every detail of Grayson's account. Still, she countered, "So you've never tried to talk your doctor out of an office call?"

"What's that got to do with anything?" Grayson blustered. Glowering, he added, "The kid couldn't have been very sick. His dorm roommate dropped in several times that day. He didn't see Sutton once. And there's more." Grayson punched his words as if banging a gavel. "Sutton admitted that he knows your code."

Not good.

"And he's behind on his tuition payments big time."

She raised her voice. "Look, just because a boy is poor—"

"Financial problems are a great motive for burglary."

"If he'd wanted to steal, why didn't he?" she asked. "The house holds a gazillion antiques, not to mention computers—"

"Would you both like coffee?" Essie offered them steaming cups. She said in a low, pleasant voice, "You might be able to discuss this better in the break room."

Of course. Shannon flushed. Only Grayson could have goaded her into an argument in her retail area.

She gestured to the chief. Instead, Grayson downed the hot coffee like a shot and said, "Too much to do. I have to go."

He banged the jangling door, leaving Shannon to fume and wonder where the skinny, nerdy boy went that day. And what secret he was trying to hide.

*   *   *

College campuses usually morphed Shannon back into a carefree coed—which inevitably embarrassed her twins when she visited them at Portland State University.

Today, however, during their lunch date, she didn't revert back to her St. Andrews days.

"I hope Chris will talk to you; he sure isn't talking to us." Alec didn't sound optimistic. "He won't answer my texts or voice mails."

"Mine either. I doubt he'll welcome me with open arms. But I have to try." Shannon kissed them goodbye. "Maybe I can keep Grayson from dragging him down to the police station."

She bundled up and donned dark glasses, then strolled along the South Park Blocks. She sat on a park bench near the front of the semicircular Millar Library with its rows of glass windows.

Lara had told her Chris always spent Friday afternoons at the library. "Crazy, but true," she said.

"That's your best bet," Alec agreed.

Shannon monitored various exits of the building. No luck. When the bleak autumn sun hid behind the clouds, she took her stakeout inside. About the time she considered going home, she spotted Chris heading for a stairway. She hurried toward him.

"Excuse me," she said in her best lost-parent voice.

"Yes?"

"Chris, I'd like to talk to you a few minutes."

The dark eyes behind the taped glasses widened. "Ms. McClain? Um, I'm busy. Really."

He headed up the stairs, Shannon at his elbow. Thankfully, most people took the elevators, so perhaps she could accost him in private.

His stride stretched twice as long as hers. Like Michael's.

She puffed, "I know you didn't break into my house."

Chris paused. He looked pleased, but panic soon overruled his faint smile.

"I—I'm glad," he said in a low voice.

He resumed his ascent, but if anything, he climbed faster.

Shannon said in desperation, "We need to talk. The police chief wants to throw you in jail."

Chris turned, his face waxy. "There's no evidence to connect me with all that," he said in a weak voice.

Shannon finally caught up with the boy. "No, but if you don't tell him where you were that day, he will dog your steps."

Chris drooped like a tall, neglected plant. "I turned off my cell, just to get away from him."

"You won't." Shannon looked him in the eye.

Chris set his jaw. His volume rose. "Look, I was a little sick and skipped a class I hate. Are those federal crimes?" Now he was the one breathing like a heart attack loomed. "Where I went is nobody's business. His or yours."

"Chris, I really think—"

His chin dipped. "Sorry, I don't like to be rude. You were really nice to me last summer. But I don't have to take this hassle."

He fled up the next flight.

Shannon stared after him, trying not to imagine the worst.

— 8 —

For the first time, Shannon wished the Purls weren't meeting at her house that night.

She had pushed, pushed, *pushed* the past few days to complete numerous silver and beading projects she'd promised customers. Today's encounter with Chris exhausted her further. Only a hot, bubbly bath surrounded by scented candles sounded appealing.

Thank heaven, Joyce had volunteered to bring refreshments, since Deborah couldn't provide them. Her housekeeper had received a phone call the night before from her Aunt Maudie's nursing home, and she'd had to prepare for a quick trip to Tacoma. Before she left that morning, she called Shannon at work twice to assure her, "Don't worry. I turned on the security system."

Now, at the end of her work day, Shannon thought that climbing into Old Blue's cab felt like scaling Mt. Hood. Why hadn't her grandfather passed down his height, along with his red hair and his complications?

Her mood didn't lighten as she drove, the cold, gray twilight seeping into her bones. Even flipping a turn signal seemed like too much work.

No reading logs for you tonight, her common sense scolded. *Go to bed before midnight for a change.*

Her late hours had taken their toll. Chris's stricken face

haunted her. The stuffy secret room, now barred with a super-complex new lock—and the sofa she shoved in front of it when not in use—still drew her. She sat inside it almost every night, as if she could absorb answers from its atmosphere.

Answers about a missing map.

A Spanish doubloon.

A faceless man—or was it a woman?—who shadowed her every thought.

Did he shadow her every move as well?

Michael was protecting her. She knew that as well as she knew her name. But after he'd dissed Hunter again, she didn't sense the partnership they'd shared in other cases.

As she guided Old Blue toward the garage, the sight of Joyce's delivery van parked in her driveway cheered her a little. *Maybe a Purls meeting will be good for me after all.*

"You look like you need cupcakes." Joyce pulled a large pink box with black polka dots from her van.

"Do I ever." Shannon flung a straggling curl away from her face and carried Joyce's glitzy magenta knitting bag to the house.

At the sight of the familiar grand entrance, though, she nearly dropped the bag.

The front door was open.

*   *   *

"Chief Grayson says you may now move freely throughout the main story." Officer Brownley paused. "If you wish."

Thank goodness. Shannon's lovely breakfast room had

felt like a prison the past few hours. She and the Purls stood. Shannon entered the kitchen.

And wished she hadn't.

Drawers of silverware and cooking utensils had been dumped on the kitchen floor. Pans lay scattered about as if a tornado had washed and dried them. Dishes sat in heaps on counters, many in fragments on the floor as well.

Could she stand a tour through the rest of the house?

She closed her eyes, thankful Joyce and Betty were taking pictures with their cellphones for insurance purposes.

"You shouldn't deal with this now." Betty lowered her phone. "I wish you'd let me take you to my house, at least for a while."

Shannon shook her head. She knelt and retrieved her cracked butterfly mug and its broken handle, trying to piece it together. A big glop or two of superglue might mend her favorite cup. If only it would hold her together as well ....

She wandered down the hallways to the back stairs closet. The sofa had been pushed aside.

So much for that silly precaution.

She entered and waded through piles of clothing toward the open back panel and the door to the secret room.

Still locked. At least Michael's recommendations for that had proved useful.

She backed out of the closet and headed for the dining room.

"Don't go in there." Betty blocked Shannon's path. "It's worse than the kitchen."

"I'll see it sooner or later." Shannon stared her friend down. Shaking her head, Betty stepped aside.

Shannon looked around with dismay. She saw paintings

yanked off the walls, slashed from their frames. The long teakwood table, its sections removed as if by careless surgery. Her grandmother's matching buffet, its shelves and back bludgeoned. Silverware had been tossed aside as if plastic. If the whole house looked this way, the burglar must have recruited help.

For once, Shannon was glad her grandmother no longer lived.

"Why didn't they just steal?" Shannon stroked a damaged landscape of the estate's lake as if trying to soothe its hurt. "Why did they have to destroy?"

Betty slipped an arm around her. "I think Grayson is right. The vandalism shows these thieves focused, first and foremost, on finding something."

The journal. Thank heaven she'd left it in her bank's lockbox.

She wandered back into the kitchen, grateful the police chief remained upstairs with his officers. Time with her friends might help her absorb all this without cracking.

"I wish I'd arrived earlier," huffed Joyce as she gathered pans from every corner. "Those guys would have regretted the day they were born."

"I'm so glad you didn't." Shannon scanned the devastation around her. "Sure, this makes me sick. But most of these things are repairable or replaceable." She leaned into Joyce's strong arms. "You're not."

Joyce's pillowy hug had never felt so good. "Now that we have access to the kitchen," her friend said, "why don't I fix you a nice cup of tea?"

"I'd love that."

"Those creeps threw all that food out of the freezer, looking for whatever it is." Melanie's nose wrinkled in disgust as she pointed to overflowing trash cans she'd filled. She opened the fridge. "Well, what do you know. Those vandals left a few things intact. They didn't crack the eggs, and they feel cool. I'll bet you're hungry, Shannon. How about a mushroom omelet?"

She'd forgotten supper. "Yum. Bring it on."

She let Joyce steer her into the breakfast room. Her friend found and arranged clean, colorful place mats, unbroken china, and a candle on the table, which she lit.

Melanie slid a fragrant omelet, covered with melted Havarti, onto Shannon's plate, along with one of Deborah's scones. She commanded, "Eat."

With every warm, luscious bite, strength flowed into Shannon. What would she do without her God-given friends? A prayer of thanksgiving seemed absurd, but she breathed one anyway.

Kate, who arrived breathless, as usual, brought her latest boarder. The fuzzy, gold Labrador puppy contributed a curious nose, wagging tail, and sloppy kisses to the chaos.

"Sorry I had to bring Sonny with me," Kate apologized, "especially when everything's so awful. But he's younger than most of my dogs, and I didn't want to leave him alone his first night."

Shannon, cuddling the puppy, scanned the destruction around her. "I don't think he'll hurt anything."

"Probably not." Joyce scratched his head.

The little dog licked Shannon's nose with his warm tongue, and she couldn't help giggling.

The laugh died in her throat as the voices of Grayson and his men floated from the grand stairway in the foyer. She stood, and the Purls followed her past Victoria's horse statue. It appeared minimally damaged—probably because it was solid marble. The officers descended the stairs in a solemn parade. Sonny, now carried in Kate's arms, yipped at them as if they were the criminals.

Annoyance crossed the police chief's face, but he said, "The first break-in was difficult, I'm sure, but this is much worse. The upstairs looks as bad as down here. I'm sorry."

His sympathetic words surprised Shannon almost as much as the burglary. "Thank you."

"We'll do everything we can to track these vandals."

She nodded.

"Since you insist on staying here, I'll leave an officer on duty tonight."

"We're staying too." Betty encircled Shannon with her left arm.

"You bet." Joyce hugged her from the right side, and the other Purls gathered around them. Shannon knew she had no say in the matter, and she was glad. "Thanks, ladies. But may I have a word with Chief Grayson in private?"

He gestured to his men, who exited. Shannon took him aside while the Purls retreated into the hallway.

She injected a note of pleading into her voice. "Chris Sutton couldn't have done this. I saw him this afternoon in Portland. And whatever you say, I know he had nothing to do with the first burglary—"

"He's no longer a suspect," Grayson said shortly.

"He's not?" She stared. "What did you find out?"

He grimaced. "During the burglary's time frame, another student saw Sutton at a Starbuck's off campus. She said Sutton was acting strangely, talking to someone who wasn't there.

The girl tried to help, but Sutton became so belligerent that the manager asked him to leave."

"Chris?" Shannon's jaw dropped. "He would never act like that."

"That's what the witness said." Grayson continued, "She followed Sutton from a distance to a psychiatrist's office nearby and saw him go in. Later, she expressed her concern about Sutton's behavior to his professor, the one whose class he'd skipped. The prof called me, and together we confronted Sutton. He said he'd spent the afternoon at the psychiatrist's office, and the office people confirmed that. The doctor was two hours late for Sutton's appointment because of an emergency, but the kid refused to reschedule. He huddled in a corner of the waiting room the whole time."

Poor Chris. Shannon recalled the boy's agitation when she'd tried to talk to him.

The police chief shook his head, and more than a tinge of compassion colored his voice. "He was afraid to tell his folks he was hearing voices. Said he knew they wouldn't understand. Afraid his friends who worked at the college health center would find out."

At least Chris doesn't have to go to jail. Shannon ached for the young man. *I knew he didn't break into my house.*

Grayson turned as if he wanted to change the subject. He stared at the Purls talking in the hallway and cleared his throat. When they continued their conversations, he cleared it again, loudly.

They quieted.

"We're done down here, and you can clean up if you want. Be sure to make a list of missing items." He resumed some of his usual chutzpah. "But don't disturb the upper story until we finish tomorrow, or you might destroy valuable evidence. Don't try to play detective, ladies." He eyed them as if they were third graders. "If you notice anything else unusual, tell an officer immediately. One will be on duty outside, near this entrance."

Melanie slipped in front of Shannon, smiling sweetly. "Of course we will, Chief Grayson."

The Purls breathed a simultaneous sigh of relief when the chief exited the front door.

Shannon said, "I guess I should thank Grayson for raising my spirits."

Joyce gave an incredulous snort. "You're kidding."

"No. I mean it." Shannon imitated Melanie's sweet-lady smile. "First, he irritated me so much, I almost forgot about this—this mess. Second, his leave-the-tough-stuff-to-me attitude motivates me to do something about it. And third—"

"Every time he walks out the door, you feel so-o-o much better. Yay!" Joyce jumped like the cheerleader she once had been.

"You got it, girl." Shannon joined Joyce in a boogie across the foyer. The other Purls danced, too, and Sonny barked his own hurrahs.

"Let's not get carried away, ladies. Jack Grayson is a good man." Betty cautioned when they began to wheeze. "And we've got a job to do."

Shannon protested, "It's too late to do much tonight."

"Nonsense." Betty's conquer-the-world persona had kicked in. "We certainly can't finish tonight, but we'll clear out a sane space for you."

"Who knows what we can accomplish on cupcake power!" Joyce exclaimed, retrieving her Pink Sprinkles box. She opened it to reveal rows of enormous cupcakes, frosted with pink icing and white rosettes, resplendent with filigrees of grated dark chocolate. "Double chocolate or raspberry filling, whichever suits your pleasure."

Shannon's morale, alone with that of her cleaning crew, rose considerably.

Joyce gestured with her head toward the breakfast room. "Somebody fix us a couple pots of high-octane coffee, I'll contribute the sugar, and we'll have this place in such good shape tomorrow that Grayson won't recognize it!"

*   *   *

A footstep crunched on the leaves outside. Then another.

Lying in the darkness, hair prickled on Shannon's arms. But from her sleeping bag on the cushy drawing room carpet, she spotted Officer Brownley's shadowy form as he passed the window.

She probably wouldn't enjoy the luxury of a personal guard outside her house very long. So tonight, she needed to take advantage of it and get some sleep.

Following Grayson's orders to stay out of the upstairs bedrooms, the Purls had clumped together like middle schoolers at a sleepover. Shannon glanced around the room at lumpy silhouettes. Betty occupied the second sofa, Melanie slept on a combination armchair/ottoman, and Kate had curled up with Sonny in a sleeping bag on the floor. They'd convinced Joyce, due at her bakery in only a few hours, to borrow Deborah's room.

Shannon could sleep, just like the others.

Of course she could.

An hour later, she hadn't closed her eyes.

Noiselessly, Shannon slid from her sleeping bag. Sonny's open eyes glistened in the darkness, but he didn't stir as she padded across the room. Obviously, he didn't want to leave his warm, snuggly abode.

She'd always heard dogs were smarter than people.

Shannon bypassed the kitchen and breakfast room, with their numerous windows, and sat on a wooden stool in the pantry. She pulled her phone from her sweatpants pocket.

Was Hunter a good enough friend to call in the wee hours?

She'd soon find out. Shannon hit her speed dial.

"Mmmrrrphh?"

Didn't sound promising.

"H-Hunter, I'm sorry I woke you up." *Though that's exactly what I intended.*

"Shannon?"

Now he sounded almost as wide awake as Michael would, the night owl. Shannon gritted her teeth, then babbled, "Someone's burglarized my house again—"

"You're kidding!" His outrage blared through her phone.

"I wish. This time, he tore up everything he touched." Her tears finally broke their dam.

"Shannon, I'm so sorry." His kind baritone warmed her like a blanket. "I wish I were there."

Rats. She'd forgotten he'd returned to Eureka for a few days.

He continued, "But I'll leave right now, OK?"

"You don't have—"

"I want to. Will you be at the house or the shop?"

A thrill swirled through her tired brain. "The house, probably. The police are coming again—"

"They should." Ire deepened his already resonant voice. "I can't believe they let that guy break in again. And what about that so-called security system Stone installed? You're going to fire that guy, right?"

"I—I—"

"I'm sorry. Not the time to mention that." His volume dropped. "Are you alone, Shannon?"

There was an anxious note in his voice. Almost tender.

"No. Deborah's in Tacoma, but the Purls came to help clean up and stayed the night."

"I hope they're armed and dangerous." A hint of a chuckle made her smile.

"Not like Deborah." Shannon's tiny smile grew. "But I pity the guy who would try to get past them."

"Good. I'll be there before noon, OK? Until then, please, *please* be careful."

She had been careful, but she didn't mind hearing Hunter say it. She longed for his touch, his strong arm around her. "I will. See you soon."

9

Rats. Of course he would come.

Shannon watched Michael's black Lexus zoom up her driveway through the early morning sleet.

"Great." She slammed down the toast she'd been trying to nibble. "What do I do now?"

"You tell Michael what happened." Betty, bundling up to return to her inn, gave Shannon a curious look. "He'll know what to do next."

"Yet his security system didn't prevent the burglaries." The anger that had simmered like a lava flow beneath Shannon's thin crust of sanity erupted before she could stop it. "How do I know he can do anything to keep this creep out of my house?"

Betty stopped pouring coffee into a paper cup. She put a firm hand on each of Shannon's shoulders and said quietly, "This has been impossibly hard on you. But you have to put your faith in people you can trust. People who have proven themselves." Her motherly look bored through Shannon. "Michael has done that. He's saved your life more than once."

Shannon's mouth twitched like a beached fish's, but no words came out.

"He's not infallible," Betty continued, unblinking, "but if he's made a mistake, Michael will say so. And he'll correct it."

She hugged Shannon, gave her the Betty smile that brightened the day for tired tourists, and capped her coffee.

"I'm glad Melanie doesn't have to work until noon."

"Me too." Shannon finally forced out a few words. She clung to Betty for a second. "If you and the Purls hadn't helped me, I wouldn't have survived this nightmare."

"Yes, you would."

Betty's confidence made Shannon straighten her shoulders. "OK. But it would have been a hard night."

The front doorbell rang.

"Wish I could stay, but we have a wedding booked this weekend. Tom can't prep the inn by himself." Shuddering at the thought, Betty waved goodbye as she left.

As Shannon walked to the foyer, she wished Joyce were here. From moment one, she would have blasted Michael with indignant questions about why he had let this happen. Kate, who'd gone home to feed her boarders, might have let wagging, slobbering Sonny loose on Michael—who didn't care for animals.

But Melanie, who appeared in the hallway momentarily, whisked back into the study and closed the door.

She was giving them privacy—the last thing Shannon wanted.

The bell chimed again. Shannon slowly turned the knob.

Michael burst through, sending her skittering backward on the slick marble floor.

He grabbed her by the waist and held her. "Shannon! Thank God you're all right." Strong arms around her. Not the ones she'd anticipated.

"Uh—" Her mouth was doing the beached fish thing again.

Michael set Shannon on her feet, his stricken face stiffening into a mask. "Sorry. Didn't mean to knock you down."

"I'm fine." She crossed her arms. "Just fine."

"I doubt that." A dull red crept up his slightly grizzled

G U I L T Y   T R E A S U R E S   101

cheeks. "I was in Sacramento overnight, but I heard your house was burglarized again."

Shannon nodded.

"I'm sorry." The blue-steel eyes intensified, so she dropped her own gaze to her hands.

Sorry? That's all you can say?

He said, "May I take a look?"

What good will that do? She wanted to fling the words into his face like gravel.

"Fire that guy!" Hunter's diatribe echoed through her head.

"Michael's saved your life more than once." Betty's gaze seemed to reach Shannon from her inn.

Finally, Shannon gestured with a limp hand toward the hallway. He followed her into the still-chaotic study.

They could hardly walk through decimated flocks of books on the floor. Bins of Shannon's favorite beads, yarns, and other supplies had been emptied like trash cans, their contents slung far and wide. At the sight of slashes in the beautiful cherry woodwork and shelves, her eyes teared all over again.

"This is obscene," Michael said quietly. *Exactly.* He knew how Shannon felt. Whether she wanted him to or not.

"Did he do this to the whole house?"

"I haven't gone upstairs because Grayson and his men didn't finish." Shannon fixed her eyes on an intact cushion on the sofa. "The Purls stayed with me last night. They helped make the main floor livable, but we haven't had time to clean in here."

"How about the secret room?"

"The intruder couldn't get in." Right now, she didn't care about the secret room. Shannon sank to her knees and began to pick up seed pearl beads, tiny purple agates, and

Swarovski crystal snowflake beads, the ones she'd been using to decorate a scarf for Lara for Christmas.

"Shannon."

She continued cleaning, her fingers pecking at the beads.

"Shannon, may I check out the security system?"

"If you want." *Peck, peck.*

"I want."

His footsteps exited, then headed down the hall.

Only after he'd left did cold, clear questions emerge in her murky mind.

How long would Michael's evaluation last? Would he finish before Hunter arrived?

*　　*　　*

I needed this. Shannon breathed in the fragrant mix of Espresso Yourself's mellow coffees and the spicy pumpkin candles Essie lit to brighten the gloomy day. The colorful, attractive displays in the beading, quilting, and decoupage areas salved the rawness of Shannon's pain. Amazing what the routine tasks of separating, stacking, and organizing could do for a person. She'd stayed at home until Grayson came, but he appeared more than happy to confer with Michael and wave an offhand goodbye to her.

Hunter had protested when she'd called him. "Go to work? You need to rest!"

Thank the Lord, she'd talked him into meeting her here. Actually, she wished she could spend the entire day in her lovely, pleasant shop, chitchatting with customers, feeling normal. She might even find time to work on the pink jade bracelet Mrs.

Perkinson wanted. Shannon's hands fairly ached to hold her tools, to solder and twist and etch the design into silver.

Metals and stones did not ask questions. Treated right, they responded as expected.

Not like men. She shook her head.

Gladness bubbled through her, though, when Hunter dashed into the shop as if reaching a finish line. He hugged her breathless, his face alight with relief and righteous anger. "I am taking you away from all this. Right now."

A small spot of irritation blighted her happiness at seeing him. *I want to stay.*

But how could she object, after he'd driven seven hours to be with her?

So she made only a token protest as he tucked her inside his SUV and headed for Portland on the interstate. But when the inevitable probing began with a nasty remark about Michael, she gave Hunter a basic description of the burglary and cut off further inquiry saying, "I've left it in the police's hands for now. I don't want to think about it."

"I can understand that." His soft gaze soothed her curtness. "Let's run away together and play. Why don't we go ice skating? I know of an awesome indoor rink where we'll stun the world with our triple axels."

Shannon snorted. "I haven't skated in years. I don't know if I can even stand."

"I don't either," Hunter said cheerfully. "But we'll hold each other up."

He threw her a look that made her catch her breath. She covered her emotion with "Are you sure you want to do something that strenuous? You didn't sleep much."

"Neither did you." Hunter reached and squeezed her hand.

Shannon stiffened as he changed lanes without checking first.

He countered her anxiety with his famous grin. "Relax. We both need to chill."

She couldn't help answering with a smile. "OK. We'll skate. But if we both end up in the hospital—"

"We'll enjoy a nice, long rest. Together."

As it turned out, Hunter proved to be a much better skater than he insinuated. He saved Shannon from falling umpteen times, performed goofy tricks that left her giggling, and guided them into a graceful promenade reminiscent of a couple on a music box.

By the time they had devoured an enormous Tuscan pizza, drowsiness had set in. He teased Shannon when she dozed off on the way home.

Shannon's nightmare returned, however, when they stood before her front door in the chilly rain and gathering darkness. She loved the Paisley mansion as if she'd been raised there, but now every cell in her body poised to flee. Michael was right. Nights alone were not an option. Yet she could not, would not give in to this—this monster.

"I should have worked out something before I left," Shannon murmured. She hadn't called Grayson. He must be thanking his lucky stars. She hadn't touched base with her friends. Or Michael—

"I won't let you stay here by yourself." Hunter drew her closer.

She pulled out her cell before he could propose the sleep-on-the-couch solution, but at that moment, the porch light flickered on and the door swung open.

Beth.

She reached for Shannon in a wordless hug. Shannon

said, "I didn't want to worry you."

"I know. But that's my job, right?"

"I called her." No apology in Betty's voice as she poked her head around the edge of the door. The other Purls crowded behind Beth. Sonny yapped nonstop.

Joyce called out, "Come in out of the rain."

Shannon tugged on Hunter's arm. "After all that exercise, we deserve a nice fattening cup of hot chocolate with Deborah's sugar cookies."

He sagged a little. "Actually, I'm kind of beat."

"I'm not surprised." She pecked him on the cheek. "Thanks for making a horrible day a fun one. Now go home and go to bed."

She stepped into the foyer, and Joyce closed the door behind her, a queen-size grin stretching across her face. "So sorry we interrupted."

"No you aren't." Shannon made a face at the Purls as they headed for the drawing room, clamoring for details of her day. "I'm tired too. I'm not saying another word until somebody fixes me my hot chocolate."

Beth hurried to the kitchen and appeared a few minutes later with a steaming mug. "Now, tell your mother all about it."

A flush stole up Shannon's face as the others chortled. *Sometimes I still forget I have a mother.*

"I'm teasing." Beth handed the mug to her. "I'm grateful Hunter gave you a break. It's good to see you smile."

"Where did you guys go?" Kate was not to be denied.

The others pulled out their knitting while Shannon told them about their adventures. Afterward, she discovered they'd been busy. Melanie had single-handedly morphed the study into usable condition that morning. The others had transformed Shannon's bedroom and a guest room.

"Sonny and I are staying here tonight," Kate announced.

"Me too." Beth slipped an arm around her again.

"I hate it when I get all weepy," Shannon sniffled. "But thank you. Thank you all so much."

The phone rang.

"That," Melanie said, "is probably Michael. He's called twice this evening."

On her way to the study, Shannon pulled out her cellphone. Four missed calls. All Michael.

She tried not to groan as she picked up the landline. "Hello."

"Michael Stone here." His professional voice boomed through the phone, a concrete-block quality to it. "We need to talk."

Every cell in her sagged. "Can't it wait until tomorrow morning?"

"I think that would be ill-advised."

Though Michael never wasted her time, she couldn't help wishing she'd fired him. She sank onto the sofa, closing her eyes. "Shoot."

"Looks like Deborah did turn on the system—"

"I knew that." Shannon huffed. "She told me twice before she left."

"But you didn't know this."

His tone froze her, yet flames of fear licked her insides. "What?"

"This burglar isn't your everyday scum." He took a deep breath. "I've worked security systems all over the world for more than twenty years. Whoever bypassed yours used a procedure I've never seen."

— 10 —

Shannon sank to the floor. Her fingers clutched the phone to her ear. She choked out, "Do you think he knows about the journal?"

"Maybe." Michael said, "You keep it in the lockbox, don't you?"

"Yes." If the creep was watching her, though, he knew she'd visited the bank far more often than usual.

Michael read her mind. "Be extra careful. The perp probably is tracking you."

Fear slithered around her, tightening its coils against her chest.

She fought it with everything she had. "I guess I shouldn't buy those Ferraris I had my eye on."

Silence.

"That was a joke." Imagining his humor-impaired expression supplied a twinge of satisfaction. Shannon flopped onto her back. The furlike softness of the rug reminded her of Sonny. "So what do we do now?"

"I'll keep working on the system." *Translation: I will tear the world apart to beat this guy at my own game.*

She sighed. "I'll take time off, if I have to, to finish the journal and read through more logs." The total destruction of her house had distracted her from her quest.

"Good. I'll be around."

As Shannon hung up, she asked herself if she liked that. Or did she hate it?

She didn't know.

*   *   *

"We must have hiked ten miles up this hill." Joyce panted as she collapsed beside the Simmuem. "Any sign of Smokey the Bear? Maybe he'll eat us and put us out of our misery."

"Smokey doesn't eat people," Kate corrected her. "He helps them."

Shannon grinned. Kate sometimes sounded much younger than her thirty-something years.

That didn't appear to bother Aaron Saska, Kate's geologist friend. His furtive glances her way as they hiked told Shannon he saw what many guys missed: a pretty woman who scorned makeup and downplayed herself in favor of others.

Shannon had Kate to thank for Aaron's interest in their hike this morning. With the burglar possibly stalking her, Shannon had Michael check Aaron's background. So far, she'd only told him she wanted to follow in the footsteps of her ancestor. Truthfully, she'd struck out in finding Black Donald's Hand, but Aaron didn't need to know that. She had inadequate information to work with. His input couldn't hurt.

She didn't know what else to do.

"You wanted to go to the burial ground first, right?" Aaron, who had grown up exploring the area, knew it better than she did. He gestured. "About a mile in that direction. Not much higher in elevation, though."

"Thank the Lord," Joyce sputtered. "Although, with all this

exercise, I can eat a few éclairs later with a clean conscience."

Though Shannon would have liked to forge ahead, she walked beside her friend to give moral support. The sight of two ponytails bouncing before them brought a smile to Shannon's face: Kate's long, silken brown locks tied with a blue ribbon, and Aaron's straight black hair and tanned neck that spoke of his Native American heritage.

Groves of pine, spruce, and juniper blocked the ocean's brisk breezes. A beneficent sun warmed their faces as they tramped the path. No one could stay in the doldrums here, with the spicy scent of evergreens and moist earth perfuming their way.

"The House of the Eagle is that way." Aaron pointed to a smaller path branching off the trail.

"Is there a special etiquette we should follow in visiting it?"

At Shannon's question, Aaron's face crinkled in a smile. "Thanks for asking, but no. When people visit the site, it kind of tells them what to do."

How right he was. The shady spot stretched onto a broad, rocky ridge that opened to a breathtaking view of shoreline cliffs and rocks below, the ocean unfurled to the west like an infinite blue flag. Conversation faded, and Shannon walked close to the edge. She inhaled and rolled the air on her tongue, fresh as a mountain stream.

After a few quiet minutes, she asked Aaron, "No grave markers? Or are the graves located farther down the path?"

"Coastal Native Americans often buried their dead in unmarked graves," he answered, "but they also placed them in canoes and set them on ridges like this, or fastened them in large tree branches."

He smiled as their eyes rose to the treetops around them. "No new burials here for at least a couple of centuries, so little visible evidence remains. Even so, our people, the Salish, consider it a sacred place."

They hiked back to the main trail and headed south again. Shannon shifted her gaze constantly, searching for Black Donald's Hand. She paused when beach vistas interrupted the line of trees and bushes, scanning the ground above them and the rocks below.

"You're my kind of hiker." Joyce didn't seem to mind Shannon's frequent stops at all. She flopped onto the soft ground and chugged water from her metal bottle.

"What exactly are you looking for?" Aaron asked after several breaks.

Shannon chuckled ruefully. "I'm not sure. Grandfather mentioned something that vaguely resembled a hand, supposedly visible from the beach. But I haven't seen anything like that—"

"Not surprising," Aaron said. He took a swallow from his own bottle, then waved an arm at the landscape. "Earthquakes happen here all the time—throughout the whole Pacific coastline, in fact. Constant small ones. Big ones too. When did your ancestor live?"

"Late 1500s, early 1600s."

"Huge earthquake and tsunami took place around 1700." Aaron munched a handful of trail mix. "I'm surprised that landmark remained all those centuries. You say your grandfather saw this hand formation during the 1940s?"

Shannon nodded, trying to hide the fact that her hopes were sinking into her hiking boots.

"We've experienced plenty of tremors since then. Land-slides too. Could easily have toppled something like that." *Crunch, crunch.* "On the other hand, the formation could have remained intact—depending on its position, its composition, and that of the rock below it—and loose boulders could have fallen from above, landing in front of it. Those might block it from the beach view."

He gestured at the pines. "Or a tree or thicket could have done the same thing."

Why hadn't she thought of that? *Duh.* Now she had to conceal the geyser of joy that rose in her. "Thanks, Aaron. I really appreciate your help."

"No problem." He glanced at Kate, who was talking to Joyce, and grinned. "My pleasure."

They hiked for several more miles. Shannon snapped pictures of every rock configuration that might possibly fit James's description, whether hidden from beach view or not. By the time they turned around, she'd collected photos of a couple of mitten-shaped boulders sporting one thumblike projection and numerous long, cylinderlike rocks lying on the ground that once could have been attached to surrounding boulders.

It had been a long, hard trek, and nothing had shouted, "I'm Black Donald's Hand!"

When the group, tired and dirty, adjourned to the back room of Joyce's bakery for éclairs, Shannon's optimism didn't soar. But it didn't flop like an injured gull, either.

She still had no intention of revealing her treasure hunt to Aaron or anyone else unless absolutely necessary. But perhaps she might feel out his knowledge of the beach area.

Shannon wiped cream filling from her lips and asked about earthquakes' effect on the shoreline. Aaron answered that they had modified the rock structures significantly, and that in this particular area, the resulting tsunami had swept in silt, adding additional inches to the beach.

Had the tremors changed Parable Rock or Witch Cave? Shannon didn't think the small influx of silt could have covered the landmarks, but then, she was no geologist. Aaron might not be able to give her a firm answer. But he had fished in the Simmuem and climbed these hills since he was a kid. She waited until he'd swallowed the last of his third éclair, then plunged in. "My grandfather mentioned a few other places along the beach, one called Parable Rock and the other, Witch Cave."

"Never heard of Parable Rock," he said. "Nothing officially known as Witch Cave, either. But that might be—pardon the expression—the white man's name for a place the Salish call Wild Woman Waters."

Wild Woman Waters. WWW. Shannon's hopes were soaring now—approaching the top of Mt. Hood. "I'd really love to go there."

"Maybe Kate and I can take you, as finding it's a little tricky." He cast an inquiring look at Kate and smiled broadly when she nodded. He added, "I'm not free until Saturday after next, but if the weather's decent, we can plan on it."

"Awesome."

While he and Kate flirted, Shannon slipped Joyce payment for two more éclairs. Shannon handed the Pink Sprinkles box to Aaron. "Thanks for all your help. I'll look forward to our next hike."

— 11 —

"Turn down your torch, Denton!" Shannon rarely raised her voice during her silversmith classes, but the kid seemed intent on blowing them all up.

Denton squinched his chubby adolescent face in protest but turned down the acetylene torch—at least for awhile. As she demonstrated techniques, Shannon kept one eye on the boy. By the end of the lesson, she needed drugs. Strong ones.

She popped two extra-strength aspirin as she hurried to meet Beth at the Butter Clam Inn, an out-of-the-way but surprisingly large restaurant an hour or so away.

"If things don't change," she told her mother over menus and Darjeeling tea, "Denton will have to pursue a different pastime. Do you know of any school clubs for junior flamethrowers?"

Beth chuckled, but worry lines around her mouth deepened. "You don't need that kind of pressure. You've had more than your share lately."

What a week. Since the second burglary, Michael haunted the Paisley estate night and day, though he said little. Hunter hovered over her too. Fortunately, they hadn't collided again—not directly—but neither hesitated to advise her to lose the other guy.

Sadly, the inn's cozy blue-and-yellow décor and hurricane lamp lighting didn't ease her stress. Already cramping, the muscles in Shannon's neck began a tug-of-war in earnest.

"Try the clam and scallop Florentine linguini." Beth patted her hand. "Pasta is always good for what ails you."

Shannon attempted a smile. Actually, what she needed was one good night's sleep. But she had to admit her view of her world improved substantially after stuffing herself with a platter of creamy comfort.

"See what I mean?" Beth munched clam fritters, occasionally closing her eyes in ecstasy.

As Shannon mellowed, she told Beth more tales of what she'd missed while the twins were growing up in Scotland, tales of how preschool Lara had trimmed both Alec's and her curls to nubbins and how Alec had terrorized his teachers with fireworks. "How I dreaded those calls from his school."

Beth laughed until she wiped her eyes. The crevices around her mouth faded, and Shannon saw again how much Lara resembled her grandmother.

Beth said little about Gourmet on the Go's business problems, but Shannon knew they weighed heavily on her. She promised herself she would grab the bill, if she had to arm-wrestle her mother for it.

She started to gesture to their waiter as she sipped the last drops from her teacup but nearly dropped it.

Hunter.

She hadn't noticed the large mirror on the opposite wall until his reflected smile fastened on her and turned her head. Shannon inhaled. He must be sitting behind them.

With a lovely Asian girl.

"What's wrong?" Beth leaned forward, her voice hushed. "And don't tell me 'nothing.'"

Shannon wet her lips. "I can see Hunter in a mirror. He's sitting behind me, near the lighthouse quilt on the wall."

"Is he with someone?"

Shannon nodded, fighting the absurd fury boiling in her too-full stomach. "I shouldn't be upset. We haven't agreed to date each other exclusively."

"I'll move so I'm less visible," Beth whispered. She shifted farther back in the booth. She leaned her head on her hand, tilting her head so she could observe the couple. She did it so naturally, so unobtrusively.

Despite Shannon's chagrin, she wondered how many times her mother, a former journalist, had observed goings-on with that casual air. Lacking tea, Shannon gulped water from her water glass to douse the fire in her gut. She fumbled in her navy-and-olive beaded bag for her billfold.

After several minutes, Beth spoke. "If I were you, I wouldn't jump to conclusions. This appears more a business encounter than a romantic one."

Right. Shannon made herself study the couple. Hunter's charisma had kicked into high gear. The woman with the long, shining black hair spoke in low, clipped words. His boyish grins didn't seem to affect her, nor did the melting timbre of his voice as it rose and fell. Though he appeared charming as ever, his eyes didn't match the smile on his lips.

Maybe Beth was right. Shannon strained her ears, but the dining room buzz drowned out the words.

Hunter opened his hand on the table. A glimmer of gold escaped. Then he laid it on the table.

A coin.

Shannon caught her breath. And the word "map."

Could this be her grandfather's doubloon, the one that indicated the treasure was near?

The Asian woman examined the coin. Shannon fought the urge to run and grab it from her.

Her rational side protested. She needed far more evidence than this to draw any conclusions. Surely Hunter could explain this little vignette. Perhaps he sold coins on the side.

Funny that he'd never mentioned it to her.

Beth's jade gaze rested on her. "What do you want to do?"

"Leave. By the side door."

Beth nodded. Shannon motioned for their bill, ignoring her mother's protests even as she tried to hide her relief. After paying, they slipped out.

Shannon motioned to Beth. "Could you come sit in my truck awhile? I need your help."

"I don't know why you keep that hideous old relic," Beth said, but she followed Shannon to Old Blue in the deepening twilight.

They scaled the high seats. Shannon turned on the ignition and the rumbly heater to ease their shivers. She faced her mother. "I know you want nothing to do with the treasure—"

"Absolutely." Beth straightened. "That treasure, real or imaginary, has created nothing but pain and trouble." The parking lot lights revealed only the lower portion of Beth's face, but her mouth had thinned to a firm line. "Surely you don't think Hunter is involved with the burglaries, just because he possesses a gold coin and mentioned the word 'map'?"

"Or because he's with another woman?" Shannon threw back. "Maybe you believe I'm thinking with my heart instead of my brain?"

Beth dropped against the seat back. "I don't know what to think."

"I don't either, but I want to find out." Shannon massaged her aching forehead, wishing she'd brought more aspirin. "I *have* to find out."

"You're more like me than you care to admit." Beth kneaded the back of her neck. "May I remind you what my 'have to find out' did to our family?"

Shannon fell silent. Years before, Beth's journalistic quest to expose the Scottish mafia, the Camorra, resulted in death threats, blackmail, and her secret exile far from her husband and preschool-age Shannon.

On the other hand, if Shannon didn't solve the mystery of the map, would she ever feel safe again? Her eye wandered to a dark green Jeep Grand Cherokee parked on the other side of the lot, similar to Hunter's. "Help me keep watch for a bit," Shannon pleaded. "If they came together, may I borrow your car to follow them? Hunter knows Old Blue—"

"Not the best car to tail someone with." Beth nodded, despite her chagrin. "All right—though if they go to her apartment or his, you might find yourself in an—um— embarrassing situation."

Shannon's stomach churned. "I'll take that chance. If they drove separately, I'll follow the woman in Old Blue."

Beth sighed. "I suppose you'd like me to follow Hunter?"

"If you would, please." Shannon realized she sounded like Lara asking for spending money.

"All right. But only because I love you."

Shannon's heart constricted. "Thank you."

Beth shifted in her seat. "If we're going to make this

Chinese fire drill happen, we'd better focus."

They monitored the restaurant's exits. Shannon realized they both were leaning forward, hounds on a scent. *Beth's right. We are more alike than I thought.*

"There they are." Shannon slid her finger along the dashboard below the window to point to the couple. "West exit."

The woman's black hair gleamed against the silvery little hat she wore. Shannon braced herself to witness a goodnight kiss. But Beth's hunch about a business relationship appeared correct. The couple exchanged a few terse words, Hunter threw out one last dazzling smile, and they headed to separate cars. And yes, he aimed his remote at the green SUV.

Beth pushed the passenger door open and slid to the ground. "Call me."

Her mother hurried to her elderly sedan and pulled away almost before Shannon realized she'd gone.

Shannon noted that the Asian woman entered a sporty black car two rows adjacent to hers. Hunter's dinner partner headed toward the nearest parking lot exit. Shannon steered Old Blue toward the other. Essential to put space between them, but trying to watch before and behind, Shannon almost rammed an indignant older couple's coupe. She flushed with humiliation, mouthing an "I'm sorry." Why didn't these kinds of hiccups happen in the movies?

Old Blue barely chugged to the exit in time for Shannon to see the woman's car zoom toward the interstate.

Shannon floored it. Coughing and complaining, Old Blue finally gathered speed. Shannon thanked the Lord for traffic at the freeway's junction. Congestion slowed the woman's progress, positioning Shannon and Old Blue seven or eight cars behind her.

The woman turned onto the Portland ramp. Shannon had figured as much.

Tailing Mystery Woman on the interstate didn't present a huge challenge.

Chasing her around downtown Portland proved to be another matter. As did zipping blindly around the curves of an unfamiliar parking garage designed to obliterate its customers. Finally parking on the top floor, Shannon ran to the railing and spotted the silvery hat bobbing among others on the sidewalk below. After waiting a few seconds for the elevator, she gave up and raced down flights of steps. Plunging out the door, she swiveled her head, scouring the area for the hat. Its glimmers, reflecting the street lights, caught her eye as the woman entered a glass-and-steel skyscraper at a nearby intersection. Shedding all pretense, Shannon dashed toward it.

Thanks to Zumba, she might survive this Olympic race.

Cars and drivers screeched as she sprinted across a busy street.

Maybe not.

Finally, Shannon reached her goal alive.

She sucked in deep breaths to quiet her heaving frame. A few swallows to wet her desert mouth, a brush of her hand through her hair, and she entered through the glass doors as if readying for an evening business meeting. Several people carrying briefcases lingered in the lobby.

Directly across from Shannon, behind an elliptical granite fountain, a restroom door opened. The mystery woman stepped out.

Shannon barely swallowed a cry. So much for staying inconspicuous.

But the woman glided to the elevator without a backward glance. Shannon followed. When her target pressed the "seven" button, Shannon pressed "six." Despite herself, she cast a few glances at Hunter's dinner partner. Ripe, full lips. Long, elegant legs.

Strictly a business encounter? Shannon chewed her lip. Maybe on this woman's part. Shannon doubted any man could regard it that way.

The doors *zwooped* open, and Shannon stepped out. She waited for the elevator to close, then charged up a nearby staircase and peeked out its tiny window. No one. She eased the heavy door slightly open. Another *zwoop*. She flattened her back against the door. The silver hat slid past the window. Shannon didn't breathe or move until the *tap-tap* of shoes faded. When she finally peered into the glossy, tiled hallway, she saw no one.

Shannon debated. Should she zigzag through the floor, ducking into recessed doorways, and search for her? She'd probably already entered an office.

Or should she remain in her hiding place and see which office the woman would exit?

Shannon opened the door another inch and scanned the elevator area. A lone mustard-colored chair beside a plant. She saw security cameras niched in the ceiling, aimed up and down the halls. Why hadn't she thought of that when she charged through the front door and rode the elevator?

But if she hadn't, Mystery Woman might have disappeared forever. Shannon scoured the stairwell for cameras. None visible. She let the door inch almost shut. For the next hour and a half, she alternated positions on either side of the window. A tall, muscular security guard wandered past, and Shannon breathed a sigh of relief. Remaining hidden in the stairwell had been the right choice.

She hadn't dressed for a stakeout, and the slight pinch of her new russet boots grew to pain status. She couldn't shed them. What if she had to make a dash for it? At least, the throbbing kept her awake. Ten thirty, and M.W. hadn't appeared yet. Shannon yawned. Again. She stretched occasionally, but her neck and back reminded her in no uncertain terms that they objected to this eternal vigil.

Och! I could be home looking through logs. Instead of closing in on the treasure, Shannon might wait for the fashionista floozy until she suffered permanent paralysis.

The hallway lights dimmed. But they found M.W.'s hat as she emerged from an office several doors down. Shannon flattened against the door again and watched the woman pass. When the elevator closed, she considered a quick trip down the hall to scrutinize the office M.W. had entered. But she'd better try that during the day, when she could fade into the business crowd—perhaps pretend she'd wandered into the wrong office.

Shannon plodded down the stairs to the main floor. Side exit or main doors? Since the cameras already had recorded her presence, acting like a regular in the building might make her stand out less. Shannon left by the main doors. She didn't encounter M.W. on the street or in the parking garage.

Once in the car, she texted Beth that she was fine and would call her tomorrow. Shannon fought sleep all the way home.

It fled, however, when she checked her voice mail.

A honeyed message from Hunter, cooing he couldn't wait to see her again.

*   *   *

The creamy seafood chowder slipped from the thermos cup down Shannon's throat—almost as easily as Hunter's deception had.

That is, if he were lying to her.

"Don't you like it?" He cocked his head, little-boy dismay flooding his face. He twisted the ring on his finger.

"It's delicious." She finished it off, coaxing a smile to her lips. Not difficult on this magically warm fall day. The benign ocean lapped the rocks where they sat, sharing a beach picnic he'd made himself. Especially with the sun and wind running their fingers through his thick, sandy hair, teasing her to do the same.

"That's better." He touched her cheek. "This burglary business is running you into the ground. Stone hasn't done diddly to protect you. And why hasn't that rocket-scientist police chief arrested the kid responsible?"

Shannon ignored the reference to Michael. "I wish the newspaper hadn't mentioned Chris as a 'person of interest' in the first place." She frowned. "Grayson himself told me the boy had valid alibis. Chris did not break into my house. Of course, the paper will never publish that."

She shook her head in the breeze, as if letting it blow through her hair could cleanse her mind of all worries and suspicion.

Maybe she shouldn't have done that. Hunter slipped an arm around her waist, drawing her closer than she knew was wise.

He breathed into her ear. "Today, let's concentrate on you. On us."

Shannon poked Hunter under his rib, his most sensitive "tickle spot." He laughed and gasped as she dashed for a long stretch of rocky sand. Already he rose to chase her, but at least she'd bought time to think of a new distraction.

She needed space to find answers for the questions that refused to keep silent.

— 12 —

The granite fountain in Mystery Woman's building splashed serenely in the afternoon sunlight. Shannon strode through the lobby doors, carrying a briefcase. She rode the elevator to the seventh floor, craving facts about M.W., but also looking forward to an evening with her twins and Beth. She hoped her business here would prove productive and brief. She exited the elevator, her face business-neutral, though her heart thudded with each high-heeled step.

The hall appeared almost as empty as the night she'd hid in the stairwell. She sat in the mustard-colored chair, dug into her briefcase for manila folders, and pulled out her phone as if consulting notes. After several minutes, she rose, continuing to "check" her phone and keeping a slow pace so she could study each office.

"Western Pacific Solutions" read the bronze letters on the first glass door. No sign on the second office; only "715" over its door. Another door read "Willamette Valley Consultants" with an idealized Mt. Hood logo.

What kind of solutions? What sort of consultants? A potential customer couldn't deduce much from these company names. Shannon walked past two more doors with vague titles and reached Mystery Woman's office, Room 718.

No name. No sliver of light at the bottom of the door. She paused and turned the doorknob. Locked, she had entered here. Shannon was sure of it.

Shannon continued down the hall to the next office, where the Wilson Foundation was housed. In contrast, this office appeared well-lit and welcoming. A young, trendy-looking receptionist with hair almost as red as Shannon's greeted her with a smile.

"Good afternoon." Shannon summoned her professional mode. "I'm Stephanie Jones of Elkland Enterprises. I'm to make a presentation to Neptune Systems, which I thought was located next door in Room 718. But the office appears closed. Do you happen to know when they'll return?"

The girl shook her head. "I'm sorry, but no one uses that office except for storage. I've never heard of Neptune Systems."

Shannon inserted a slight note of indignation into her voice. "Oh, I'm sure I heard correctly when I spoke with Mr. Brown—"

"Perhaps you're on the wrong floor." The receptionist tapped her computer keyboard. "No, no Neptune Systems. Maybe you're in the wrong building."

Her mouth smiled, displaying perfect whitened teeth, but did her eyes take on a hooded look?

"I'll recheck the address with my home office. Thanks for your help." Shannon turned to go, feeling the woman's gaze follow her out the door.

Shannon searched the rest of the hall for the imaginary Neptune Systems, mentally noting names and locations to record on her phone once outside the building. She'd feed these to Michael. Perhaps he'd discover a lead to Hunter's coin, maybe even to the treasure and the burglaries.

Or perhaps she'd just followed his latest coin customer to a dead end.

*   *   *

"Not fair." Alec's voice squeaked as if he were thirteen. "Not fair, Gram!"

Beth chuckled wickedly. Shannon shook her head as her mother finished laying all seven of her Scrabble letters on the game board, framed by a j and an e.

"Juxtapose!" Lara cried. "Has anyone in the history of the world played that word?"

"With the x on a triple letter space? I doubt it," Shannon said, surveying her own letters. Hopeless. "I can't play even one tile this turn."

She, Beth, and the twins wrangled and argued. Their game night at Beth's house nearly disintegrated when Alec consulted the online rule book for the tenth time, but Shannon savored every squabble.

Five years ago, we didn't even know my mother lived.

Tonight, in Beth's funky, colorful bungalow, three generations bickered over Scrabble. When Shannon thought of how, in her festered pain, she'd pushed Beth away, she gave thanks that her mother refused to quit on their relationship.

"You don't have to leave just because I won." Beth tried to lure the twins with more of her incredible cranberry macadamia oatmeal cookies.

They still left—taking a supply with them.

"I bet they both have dates." Shannon munched on another cookie, casting an appreciative eye at Beth's sea-themed decoupage table.

Beth glanced at her kitchen's twelve-legged octopus clock. "Only ten o'clock on a Friday? For them, the night's just begun. Maybe for us too, if we can stay awake." She grinned as she poured them each a second cup of Earl Grey.

Shannon ventured, "I've been studying Grandfather's journal lately."

Beth stiffened. "Find anything interesting?"

"He was something of a prodigal, wasn't he?"

Long pause. "That's the polite term for it."

"He refers to himself that way." Shannon covered her mother's hand with her own. "I don't like to upset you, but if I understand Grandfather better, his journal will make more sense. I'll solve this mystery faster—"

"You mean you'll find the treasure faster." Beth's face flushed a dull red. "You sound just like him."

"Beth, this treasure appears to be connected to the burglaries. I won't solve one without the other." Shannon leaned across the table, trying to capture her mother's eye. "Believe me, I'm not dreaming of a billionaire lifestyle. Any treasure I find becomes, by law, the property of the state of Oregon. Besides, the doubloon is Spanish. National and even international law might claim sovereignty."

Beth's head snapped up. "You're sure of that?"

Shannon nodded. "I checked with my lawyer. And I intend to obey the law."

Shannon felt Beth's fist, resting under her hand, slowly relax.

"I'm sorry." The faintest of smiles tugged at Beth's mouth. "It's unfair of me to assume the treasure will indenture you as it did Father."

"I can't say the mystery doesn't intrigue me." Trying to hide her interest would prove futile, Shannon knew.

"You're too much a Paisley."

"And you aren't?" Shannon marveled at her mother's thickening brogue.

"I paid far too big a price to chase my dreams of changin' the world."

"I'm not trying to change the world." Shannon leaned her head on her hand, her last drop of energy draining away. "I just want to catch whoever's breaking into my house."

Beth slid into the chair beside her and encircled her with an arm, murmuring, "I'm sorry, Shannon. Poor lassie."

Shannon leaned on her shoulder. All those years, how she'd longed for a mother's hug ...

When they reached for their mugs again, Beth made a face. "Cold. I guess we lost track of time."

"I don't mind." Shannon warmed their mugs in the microwave and set Beth's in front of her.

Her mother said, "I'm not sure I can be of any real help in this 'treasure hunt,' but I'll try."

Elation swelled in Shannon, but she curbed her eagerness out of respect for Beth's feelings. "Perhaps you could tell me a bit more about Grandfather. But first ... you should know he loved you."

Beth's demeanor shifted abruptly. "How could you possibly know that?" she snapped.

"Because he wrote it in his journal. His last entry. He even said he sought the treasure for your sake."

"I seriously doubt that." Green flames shot from Beth's eyes, burning away all traces of the gentle mother who'd cuddled her. "Did he even mention me or my mother in the rest of his precious journal?"

"Yes, he did."

"Often?"

"Um—"

"Of course not. He would return after a voyage, shower us with gifts and attention for two days, then disappear—if not literally, then emotionally." Beth spat out the words.

What could Shannon say? In James's journal, he followed that exact pattern—periodically he mentioned Victoria, the "beautiful queen of my heart," and Beth, his "red-haired angel," both of whom vanished from his sentences and thoughts for months afterward. Other women's names—Helen and Marie—appeared more often.

"Mostly, Father loved himself—and flirting with danger—more than anything." Beth thumped her mug down so hard the table shook. "If illegal, so much the better. Or at least that's how I got it from your grandmother."

"I wondered—"

"I don't know what he transported on that ship of his, but the police showed up on our doorstep several times," Beth growled, her eyes rabid. "I suppose he doesn't mention that?"

"Not directly, no."

"He tried to tell Mother and me they were his friends, seeking help in tracking down smugglers." Beth snorted. "Everyone in Apple Grove thought he was such a hero because of the war. But he excelled only because he loved to hunt the enemy, fight and win. The truth is, Father was a pirate at heart. I wouldn't be surprised if he would do anything to find the treasure. *Anything.*"

Beth's chest heaved. She didn't seem to notice the tears that had trickled down her face. Shannon pulled a tissue from her bag and touched her mother's cheek.

The small gesture seemed to break the spell. Beth's head bowed. "Oh, Shannon, I wanted tonight to be special." Her voice trailed off in a sob.

"It is special." Now Shannon comforted Beth. "The twins actually sacrificed an evening to play Scrabble with us. I bet they don't underestimate you again."

A tiny grin stole across Beth's face.

Shannon continued, "We're together, and I've learned more about you." She grabbed another cookie. "Plus, these are the best I've ever eaten. May I have the recipe?"

Beth nodded. "I don't share my recipes with just anyone. Only family."

The word vibrated between them and filled the kitchen with a quiet warmth.

I don't have to play detective every minute of every day. Shannon decided to keep her remaining questions short and to the point. She asked if her mother had ever heard her grandfather mention Black Donald's Hand.

Beth blinked. "No. I'm sure you know Scots call the devil by that name. I don't remember any landmarks with Scottish names in the area, let alone that one."

Shannon nodded. "I asked Deborah too. Her family's lived in Apple Grove for generations, but she's never heard of it. But Grandfather wrote that his ancestor Angus feared the Oregon coast more than a storm at sea. He said that 'Black Donald's Hand held all the land in his evile grip.'"

Beth shrugged. "Scots of that era were particularly superstitious. Especially when it came to the unknown."

"True." Shannon thought for a moment. "But according to the map, Black Donald's Hand lines up with Parable Rock, where Grandfather found the gold doubloon. And Parable Rock is near Witch Cave. He seemed to think that was where the treasure was hidden."

"I can't recall Father mentioning any of those." Beth frowned. "But then, he didn't talk to me about the treasure when I was little. Anything I learned, I overheard. By the time he died, I'd more or less tuned him out." She smiled apologetically. "I'm not helping you much, but did you want to ask me anything else?"

"Not right now." Shannon had probed her mother's remembrances enough. She steered the conversation toward Alec and Lara. They spent the rest of the evening chatting about the twins' eventual postgraduation plans. Both wanted to stay in the U.S. Alec planned to study law, and Lara hoped to snag a theater internship, then make her mark as an actress.

Shannon glanced at the octopus clock. "Eleven thirty? Time to go home."

"Stay here tonight," Beth urged. "It's so late—"

"I'll be fine." Shannon hugged her. "It's mostly freeway home. Deborah's back, you know, so I won't be by myself. I shouldn't leave her alone at the house either."

She'd forgotten about that. Shannon knew Michael probably hovered near the estate—he'd taken to wandering outside a couple of times per night—but her foot wanted to floor the accelerator anyway. Before long, she'd zoomed out of the city into the rural Willamette Valley, surrounded by black mountains. A pale moon wearing ragged, dark-cloud draperies followed her like a lost soul.

Her phone exploded the silence. Shannon nearly leaped through Old Blue's roof.

"Please don't say you've locked your keys in your car," she begged her children from afar. "Or that you've had a flat tire."

Even so, the thought made her grab the phone instead of letting it go to voice mail.

An unfamiliar number flashed on the screen. But since she'd cut off talkative—and extravagant—Lara's service, her daughter used disposable cells. "Hello?"

"Ms. McClain?"

Not Hunter's voice. Not Michael's. Shannon sucked in her breath.

"You've been entirely too inquisitive lately—"

"Who is this?" Shannon gritted her teeth to keep her jaw from trembling.

"Not important. What's important is that you mind your own business. Or else."

— 13 —

"What do you mean, 'don't throw so hard'?" Joyce glared at the bowling alley owner.

Just what Shannon needed: a Friday Night smackdown, Ms. Power versus Mr. Persnickety. Shannon, who'd just retrieved her ball, wished it would fall through the floor, taking her with it. "Joyce—"

"You may roll your ball as hard as you wish, ma'am." The skinny, prematurely balding owner tried to soothe her irate friend. "But when you loft it like a cannonball, it makes craters in the alley when it lands. Very expensive to fix—"

"You mean your alley can't take a little bounce or two?" Joyce looked like she wanted to toss the ball at *him*.

Shannon stepped toward them, but Betty beat her to the peacemaking position, edging a red-faced Joyce away from the guy. "Don't worry. We'll practice with her. She just needs a little adjustment in her technique."

"Well, all right." The owner looked as if he were already tallying up repair bills. "But please, no more craters. Do I make myself clear?"

The Purls—except for Joyce—nodded.

Muttering, the man headed for another group whose children were rolling multiple balls down an alley.

"What good is bowling if you can't vent your frustrations a little?" Joyce demanded. "I've had it up to here with bridezillas who demand perfect wedding cakes and don't want to pay for them."

"I feel like denting a few alleys myself." Melanie patted her on the back. "After those bridezillas left Pink Sprinkles, they visited me at the flower shop."

"I'd rather deal with dogs any day." Kate, who could charm any canine alive, coaxed Joyce into an impromptu bowling lesson that resulted in a spare—minus craters.

Thank the Lord. Shannon stretched before she aimed her ball. This bowling date was supposed to relax the Purls, not result in a lawsuit.

Or an arrest. Out of the corner of Shannon's eye, she spotted Grayson, his wife, Ann, and another fiftyish couple, two lanes over. Despite Shannon's dismay, she chuckled inwardly at her kindergarten reaction: How could the police chief be out of uniform? Grayson was wearing jeans and a surprisingly classy newsboy cap. He didn't look thrilled to see Shannon, but he raised his thick eyebrows to acknowledge her. Ann waved a cheerful greeting.

Shannon smiled at Ann and waved back. *Rats.* The police chief's very presence reminded her of the burglaries. At least he'd shown up after Joyce's altercation with the alley owner. Hopefully, Shannon and the rest of the Purls could keep Joyce corralled.

Between frames, Shannon tried to pretend Grayson didn't exist, but his bowling style intrigued her. He crept up to the line like a jungle cat stalking its prey. Then, with a wicked curve, Grayson slid the ball smoothly down the alley. It inevitably collected pins in a strike. Grayson didn't do victory dances, but he did pump his fist like a junior high boy.

Later, when she was searching the racks, seeking a lighter ball, he tapped her on the shoulder and apologized when she jumped. "Sorry. Didn't mean to scare you."

Shannon said, "No problem."

"You OK? Seen anything odd lately? I've had the guys patrol your place every night."

Concern tinged his usual bulldog growl.

"Thanks, I appreciate that. I'm fine." She probably should tell Michael about the phone call before she told Grayson.

His dark eyes squinted and probed hers. He said curtly, "We're making progress on the case, so don't go sticking your nose into trouble, all right?"

He turned before she could explode. *Just when I thought you were human.*

Shannon blasted a strike that reverberated through the alley and inside her bones.

"Woo-hoo!" Betty high-fived her as she returned to her seat. "You're ready to bowl with the big boys!"

"I'll stick with the girls." Shannon turned away from Grayson and his offbeat delivery. She chatted with Betty, enjoying the everydayness of their conversation, until Betty said, "Any new developments?"

Shannon angled away from her friend's kind but sharp blue gaze. "Mostly same-old, same-old."

"Mostly?"

"Your turn," Shannon said.

Betty bowled a strike, but after her "Yesss!" dance, she dropped beside Shannon again. "What's up?"

"Not much I can put my finger on." *I'm telling the truth. Sort of.* Shannon babbled on, "I have Michael checking a few things for me. I want to hear his results before I share them."

At Michael's name, Betty looked relieved, as Shannon knew she would. "Well, all right, but keep us posted."

Guilt niggled Shannon as she watched Betty coach Joyce's next turn. Talking about the phone threat made it too real. Living in panic mode had sapped her. A day or two of normalcy. That's all she asked.

Later, as they shared lattes after hours at Espresso Yourself, Kate asked about the naval expert who was examining Captain Paisley's logs.

"Captain Akiyama? He says he's found nothing exciting so far. Mostly readings that reflect Grandfather's trips."

"I like the little notes James scribbles about visiting South America and seeing old friends on the California coast. Here are my notes about his notes." Kate grinned as she handed them to Shannon, who studied them. "The only thing that caught my eye, though, made no sense."

Shannon looked up. "What was that?"

"Among his appointments, he listed 'soaper' a few times."

"What?" Did James remind himself to pick up his laundry? Shannon wrinkled her forehead. "Are you sure?"

"No, I'm not." Kate sighed. "I'm sorry, but your grandfather's handwriting is a bear to read."

"Don't I know it." Shannon mentally listed other possibilities. Souper? Sopper? Sucker? "Maybe I missed that term in the journal." Should she bother skimming through the blasted book again? At this point, she wished she could burn it.

"I haven't found anything." Melanie dug in her tote bag for her notes and handed Shannon the log she'd reviewed.

"I hope I'm not missing something important."

"Are you kidding?" Shannon rolled her eyes. "I'm still shocked you all agreed to read through these boring old books. What would I do without you? I wouldn't have lived through these past weeks, I can tell you that."

"You've been there for us," Betty answered. "We want to help get this guy."

Shannon took the logs the Purls had reviewed and distributed the ones she'd collected from Captain Akiyama. "Happy reading."

Grinning, Joyce took two. "Perfect. I need extra sleep this week."

Shannon stuck out her tongue, knowing her friend would scrutinize every word twice.

The guilt finger poked her again and continued to nag after she locked up.

All right, all right! I'll tell Michael about the phone call. Of course, it had been made either from a disposable cell or some old pay phone. Probably even Michael couldn't eke out any information from it.

But a cold, clear realization hit Shannon, stark as the moonlight on this frosty night: She'd thought she'd made zero progress in solving this case.

Someone else believed differently.

*   *   *

"I hadn't seen Shakespeare in ages. I'm glad you suggested *As You Like It*, Shannon." Hunter reached across the Salem coffeehouse's table and poured exactly the right amount of cream into Shannon's tea.

Even John, during their marriage, hadn't noticed the way she preferred her tea. Hunter apparently had been studying her.

Was that good? Her cheeks warmed. Questions chilled her heart.

"You seem quiet tonight, though." He adjusted his ring and reached for her hand, warming her cold fingers. "Things getting to you?"

"Oh, extra pressures at work." Work provided a great excuse for any anxiety she might show. "How's your work going?"

"Fairly well. I've spent lots of time compiling data, and I'll begin writing my paper soon." He leveled a mischievous, little-boy grin at her. "Great reasons to keep a marine biologist out of freezing water."

"Smart guy." Shannon smiled back, but Michael's doubts about Hunter wouldn't leave her alone.

So tired of wondering, pretending, probing. Shannon's resolve to fly off radar snapped. She pulled her hand away. "Very smart. Maybe smart enough to keep two women on the line?"

Hunter's eyes widened as if someone had shoved a gun in his back. "What are you talking about?"

She took a deep breath. "Perhaps I can refresh your memory. The Butter Clam Inn. A week ago."

His jaw dropped. "You were there?"

"I was."

Hunter shook his head. "You've got this all wrong."

"Do I?" *Let's hear your excuses now.*

"The woman you saw with me is a customer."

"A customer?"

"Yes. And if you'll stop firing little two-word bullets at me, I'll explain."

"Fine." *One word works too.*

Hunter sighed. "I love my jobs, but they're both part time, with lousy pay. Over the years, while doing research, I've discovered relics from shipwrecks, everything from pieces of figureheads to anchors, plus a growing market for them. While I don't have the background to do it full time, my deals here and there help support both me and my research."

But not the IRS, I imagine. Shannon decided not to mention international maritime law. She leaned forward, her lips parted. "So the woman I saw—"

"Heard about a coin I found on a beach in California and contacted me about it. I met with her, but she decided against it."

Shannon let herself relax in her chair. "I had no idea." *Because you didn't tell me. Or mention your "business" on your website.*

"So ... you admit you were jealous?"

If only the man didn't have such a cute smile. "I—I shouldn't have been. After all, we've never discussed dating each other exclusively."

"Would you like to?" He took possession of both her hands.

If only she could stop the tingles that spiraled up and down her spine. "I'd like that. I'd like that a lot."

*   *   *

"The last time I came, I had to turn sideways to get in. Maybe you won't." Aaron pointed at a slender opening angled between tall, sea-worn cliffs. He stepped back and huddled with Kate, who shivered in the wind.

"Wow, I can see why you wanted to show me this place, rather than tell me. I would have walked right past it." Shannon reached into her parka pocket and felt for her flashlight.

"Maybe if I inhale, I might make it through that crack." Michael surveyed it, shaking his head.

"I'll check it out first." After all the reading and pondering, Shannon could hardly wait. She passed through the crevice without difficulty. Walls of black rock surrounded her as if she stood inside a castle's roofless tower. With the surf's subdued roar in her ears, Shannon slipped and slid on slimy boulders that formed the chamber's floor. A rank smell permeated the place. But the sight of an enormous stone wart against a wall, its entrance curtained with greeny-brown seaweed, made it all worth it.

"Witch Cave!" Exultation spilled into her voice. *This might be it!*

She found a semi-level spot on one of the rocks and shined her flashlight into the hump's entrance. Not a large space. Shannon peered inside. A shifting floor of mud and gravel. Did that layer cover solid rock? She almost expected to glimpse Shakespeare's three witches, hunched over a cauldron in the back of the cave. Or perhaps a pirate's chest, half-covered with muck?

"See anything?" Michael yelled through the entrance.

"Nothing yet. But I haven't gone back into the cave."

Aaron called from outside, "If it's all right with you two, Kate and I will head back to Apple Grove."

"Sure." Shannon's delight faded a little. Aaron told her

they planned to go Portland later that afternoon—after she'd grudgingly asked Michael to accompany them. She slipped through the crevice to the outside again. "You guys have fun at the concert. I can't thank you enough, Aaron."

"Like I said, my pleasure." His white teeth flashed in a big grin. "Just remember the tide, OK? A couple of hours, and the waves will be hitting these rocks."

She and Michael waved as the couple, snuggling so close they appeared as one silhouette, faded into the fog.

Simultaneously, they faced each other, dropped their gazes, and then turned toward the cave. "I think I can make it through that gap," Michael said.

Shannon tried not to stare at him. "Um … all right."

He picked up the duffel bag of digging tools they'd brought. "I'll hand these in to you, then follow."

Not an especially polite question, but she had to ask it. "Er … what will you do if you get stuck?"

An odd grin tugged at his mouth. "You'll dig me out, of course."

Until the tide fills the cave. Then I'll dig an exit for me! She shrugged and entered again. Michael passed the tools to her, turned sideways, and wedged himself into the opening. He inhaled so deeply, a faint whistle blew between his front teeth.

She pressed her lips together to keep from laughing. He gave his large body a quick tug, and suddenly they faced each other in the clammy chamber. Alone.

Heat crept up her face, and Shannon knelt and pulled her clam-digging rake and shovel from the bag, trying to ignore her absurd reaction to the man.

"So this is Witch Cave." Michael hunkered down near the entrance, flicked on his flashlight, and swept its concentrated beam past the entrance, deep into the cavern. "Don't see anything right off. But you never can tell. Something may be tucked behind a ridge or under a rock." He peered up at Shannon. "If that cave floor is solid, I'm not sure how much digging we can do."

"I guess we'll find out." Carrying the tools and flashlight, she hunched her head and entered. Dank, dark walls closed in. She paused and brushed sweat from her forehead.

Shannon heard Michael shuffling behind her. Was he walking on his knees?

No way would she betray her fear of close spaces to him. She pushed toward the end of the cave, then discovered it was not the end. "Michael, I see a smaller corridor back here, on the left."

"Stay in the main chamber," he ordered.

She scowled and swept her flashlight beam into the dark, twisted recesses of the cramped hallway. "I want to see how far back it goes."

"When you explore passages, you need to tie a rope, so you can find your way back. We didn't bring one." Behind her, his words echoed off the walls, a hundred nagging dictates.

She hated it when he was right. Still—

Shannon turned to face him. "Would you mind rephrasing that?"

"What?" He sounded genuinely puzzled.

She repeated, "Please rephrase your latest edict, oh great Star Fleet Commander."

Silence. A vacuum so long, she wondered if he'd decided to stop speaking to her.

Then he said, "Would you please stay in the main room?

I-I'd hate for you to get lost in this cave."

"I'd hate for you to get lost finding me." She let a smile seep into her voice. "Come on, let's do what we came to do."

Michael crossed his arms. "Would you rephrase that?"

She flushed. "Please?"

"I'd be delighted. Where do you want to search?"

"Let's start here in the back of the main room."

Each chose a section. Shannon ran her hands over the walls, shifting loose stones and digging beneath them. She and Michael joined forces to move a small boulder.

She grunted with effort, but a current of excitement shot through her. "I think—I think there's a small recess behind this one."

More mud. She scraped it out, finding nothing but a hundred little stones. After an hour of scraping and digging, scraping and digging, she said, "You know, I already have to remind myself that this is a dream come true."

Michael chuckled. "If you say so."

"You're terribly agreeable, all of a sudden."

He pushed aside another big rock. "I really want to find out who's been targeting you."

His new contract to protect her didn't include digging in chilly, dark caves. Or endlessly patrolling her estate. Or putting up with her jibes.

"Thank you," Shannon said.

Like a candle, his concern brightened the darkness. She basked in it for a moment, then turned back to digging before she grew to like it too well.

— 14 —

We seemed to work well together, digging in smelly, scary caves. Shannon half-jogged beside Michael, trying to keep up with his big-guy stride. *Today? We couldn't be more out of sync.*

"This is the worst idea you've had yet." Michael scowled and adjusted his umbrella over her as they walked the flooded street in downtown Portland, where they'd met to escape Apple Grove's grapevine.

"I don't think so," Shannon said coolly. "I'll continue to date Hunter until I find hard evidence that he's connected with this mess."

"The man could be dangerous."

"I doubt it."

Michael snorted. "Because he wears khakis and looks like the lead in a middle-aged boy band? I can't tell you how many drug dealers I've arrested who had cute smiles." He flashed a too-accurate imitation of Hunter's grin.

Shannon wanted to kick up a puddle and splash him. "If he shows the least indication of violence—"

"It might be too late." Michael halted. His brooding eyes held hers.

Blast. Tingles again. If only she had remembered her own umbrella. "We're getting soaked." Shannon gestured at the blooming atrium of a nearby building. "Let's talk in there."

He shrugged. "You're the boss."

Yes, she was. And Michael had another thing coming if he thought he could run her life. They meandered among raised flower beds of yellow and orange chrysanthemums, philodendrons, and small palms until they found brown vinyl loveseats near one entrance. *Where are all the chairs in this place?*

Michael resolved the seating dilemma by taking the loveseat next to hers. "I've found out a few things about the building you explored."

She leaned forward. "Shoot."

He scrolled through data on his phone. "It's owned by an extremely wealthy Chinese businessman, Li Chung, one of several buildings he bought here in Portland five years ago. He deals in real estate more than anything else, and most of his holdings appear legitimate. But that particular building—"

"What about it?" Tingles again, but this excitement centered on the case.

Michael cleared his throat. "An inordinate number of vacancies in a highly marketable building. I've tracked several of the businesses housed there. Tangled threads. Some weave into seemingly unrelated businesses, and some just seem to disappear."

"I knew it." Shannon thumped the loveseat's armrest. "That woman is involved in some illegal operation."

"'That woman,'" Michael mimicked Shannon, "could be innocent. Unlike Hunter Banks."

Stung, Shannon retorted, "Sure. She bargains for illegally obtained coins. She visits a questionable office at night. You wouldn't think her so squeaky-clean if you'd been there. Or if you'd received that phone call—"

"What phone call?" His eyes pinned her. "When?"

Rats. She'd meant to tell him. Eventually. Shannon sighed. "The day I returned to the building—that night, on the way home from Beth's—some guy called me and told me to mind my own business."

"An unfamiliar voice, I take it."

She nodded.

"Did he say anything more?"

How she hated his knack for knowing when she withheld information. Shannon bowed her head. "He said to mind my own business—or else."

"A week." He sharpened his words into points. "You've known this a whole week, and you didn't tell me."

"I'm sorry," Shannon mumbled.

"You're paying me perfectly good money to protect you, yet you don't come clean with me."

Shannon knew she shouldn't raise her eyes, but she did.

What Michael said reflected his professional outrage.

The way his jaw worked and the pain in his eyes told her he cared about her. A lot.

Right now, with the Hunter situation, the burglaries, the treasure, and artist squabbles at work, she really didn't want to know that.

*   *   *

Shannon always prayed when she crossed Youngs Bay Bridge from Warrenton, Oregon, to Astoria, where Captain Akiyama lived. Whether she wanted to or not, the absurd words rose to her mind: *Please, God, keep the boats away.*

Don't let the bridge rise until I'm across.

Perhaps the craziness of the past few weeks deepened her plea. But the sun's friendly face over the picturesque town built into the hills and the sparkles on the water eased her tensions—until she realized she was comparing its blueness to the color of Michael's eyes.

Why can't the man keep his nose—and his eyes—out of my life?

Shannon chided herself. That couldn't happen soon. Shouldn't happen soon. She needed his expertise and, yes, his protection until they tracked down the burglar and possibly the treasure.

But today, she would take the captain's logs to Akiyama, retrieve others, and then forget about Michael, about everything for a few hours. She made a mental date with herself to check out the Scandinavian shops in Astoria, something she'd never made time to do.

She pulled in front of Akiyama's pleasant cottage with its breathtaking view of the Columbia River and lugged her box of books to the door.

"Come in, come in." The diminutive but erect retired navy officer and his quiet, sweet wife welcomed her with the best tea she'd ever tasted.

He hadn't, however, found any surprises in the logs he'd reviewed. "Well-traveled courses to ports primarily along the western North and South American coasts. No unknown desert islands. All very routine."

"Not very exciting reading, I imagine." If only Shannon's life were as boring as the logs.

"Believe it or not, I enjoy reviewing them." Captain

Akiyama's dark eyes twinkled. "Historically interesting, and they keep my brain cells moving."

After exchanging logs, Shannon spent a couple of hours exploring Astoria's downtown, studying Aarikka jewelry and sampling Norwegian almond *kringler* cookies. The beautiful day drew her to the Astoria Riverwalk.

No need to hurry home yet. Why not take a bike ride? All day, Shannon had heard the muffled barking of sea lions. One helpful shop owner told her she could see plenty of them near the water, especially toward the eastern end of the Riverwalk, several miles away.

She rented a bike and helmet and pedaled down the wide asphalt path, past hotels and marinas crowded with colorful boats of every size and shape. She drank in the majesty of the mighty Columbia and huge ships and barges that floated by, foghorns blaring in the crisp autumn air. Shannon encountered clusters of sea lions sooner than she expected, sunning themselves on piers, mingling their lazy barks with the comic squawks of birds perched on pilings. Other riders and pedestrians greeted her, and the approaching old-fashioned trolley, which ran alongside the Riverwalk, emitted friendly *ding-dings* as it passed.

Shannon wanted to pedal forever in this relaxing paradise. After a pleasant, wandering stop along the shoreline, however, she realized she'd lost track of time. The sun's smile was fading fast. Not only should she return before dark, but she faced a three-hour drive home. Shannon stopped, turned the bike around, and paused to wave at a few passing cyclists, envying their carefree demeanor.

Though flavored by the approaching twilight's sherbert

colors, the ride back didn't taste quite as good. Her legs reminded her they'd also covered downtown before this excursion, and questions she'd ignored all day leered from lengthening shadows.

Who called me? How did he get my cellphone number?

Is Hunter a criminal or only a charming con man?

How many caves will Michael and I search before we find the treasure?

Or would they, like Grandfather, never find it?

Like hitchhikers, the questions jumped onto the bike and weighed her down. A familiar but unwelcome twinge of paranoia made her cast a look over her shoulder.

No bogeymen with fangs. Only another cyclist several hundred feet behind her. Shannon rolled her eyes. Actually, she'd waved to him back at her turnaround. She remembered his mirrored sunglasses—

Why is he still wearing sunglasses?

And why did he turn around too?

Shannon's breath and her knees froze. She demanded they keep moving. *Don't be ridiculous. This is a public path.*

Now her body wanted to set Olympic cycling records, but she forced herself to maintain a moderate speed, only slightly above her earlier pace.

Thankfully, she was approaching the more populated part of the trail. Soon she'd reach downtown and take the bicycle back. Shannon argued with herself, but finally aimed another glance behind her.

No one. She exhaled, exasperated and relieved. The guy probably was eating supper by now. Her famished physique reminded her to stop at a drive-through before heading home.

Shannon pedaled into downtown minutes before the bike shop closed. Jumping off, she checked the quiet side street. No traffic. She wheeled the bike off the curb.

Double hamburger or triple? Big order of fries? Or a side salad to offset red-meat guilt?

A car's roar and laser headlights blasted her pleasant debate to rubble. She yanked the bike back, but a battering-ram blow sent her airborne into pain-soaked blackness.

— 15 —

Shannon opened her eyes. Light stabbed them, and with a moan, she shut it out. "Where am I?"

"Sweetheart." Beth stroked her face as if she were made of porcelain. "Thank God, you're awake."

Shannon ached all over. Even her eyelids hurt. Still, she forced them open a slit. For a moment, Shannon reveled in her mother's touch, the soft bed, and just being alive. Then her gaze wandered to the neutral walls. A white curtain hung from the ceiling.

A hospital. She'd hated hospitals, ever since John died. And she'd spent more than her fair share of time in them since moving to Apple Grove.

"You had an accident yesterday. You're at Columbia Memorial, here in Astoria. But you're going to be all right."

Shannon wet her lips. "I don't think … it was … an accident."

Her mother's eyes blanked, questioned. Then horror drew Beth's hand to her mouth.

"What was it then?" A man's deep voice. One that often sparked Shannon's temper. But when Michael emerged from behind the white curtain, sweet relief wafted through her like a summer afternoon breeze.

Shannon said, "I believe you were right. I underestimated the danger. And I should have told you I was leaving town."

He didn't reply, only shook his disheveled head. Gray

and black whiskers grizzled his face, and bloodshot eyes confirmed to Shannon that she'd probably kept him up all night.

She told Michael about the mirror-shaded cyclist and the out-of-nowhere car that struck her down. He clenched his jaw and cords in his neck grew taut. Beth uttered unfamiliar Gaelic expressions, but Shannon understood all the same.

Talking had exhausted her, but she had to know. "Who found me?"

"You were lucky." Michael laughed mirthlessly. "An off-duty EMT named Art Baker discovered you lying beside the street."

God had rescued her. She knew it like she knew her name. *Thank You.* "I'll have to ask the police how to contact him so I can tell him how grateful I am."

"Me too." Beth held Shannon's hand to her cheek.

"Might have been much worse if he hadn't found you as quickly as he did. You were going into shock." A gray-bearded, distinguished-looking man had entered without Shannon's notice. He extended his hand. "I'm Dr. Goddard. I'm sure you're well aware you have some nasty bumps and bruises."

"Yes, I figured that out."

He nodded. "A couple of cracked ribs too. We want to keep an eye on you for a day or so."

"I can rest at home—"

"No way." Beth crossed her arms. "You'll stay here if I have to chain you."

"Good. Then I won't have to do it." Michael followed suit.

"It's unanimous." Dr. Goddard's kind smile didn't change. But his words echoed with finality.

Three against one? Not fair. But maybe best. "OK."

After the doctor examined her and said goodbye, Beth

said, "The Purls are bringing the twins to visit after their last classes. We made them wait until the doctor cleared you for visitors."

"The police will want to talk to you soon," Michael said. "Grayson probably will call you too."

Shannon winced. "I can hardly wait."

"Tell him everything, Shannon," Michael urged. "I know he ticks you off, but he's one of the good guys. He needs to know details."

"I'll tell him." Shannon sank back into her pillow.

"Later." Beth plumped it a little. "Right now, this popular lady needs a nap."

"So do you. Go find a hotel and sleep." Michael looked as tired as Beth. But his tone left little room for objections. Beth held Shannon gently, kissed her lightly, and left.

Shannon smothered an "Ouch!" as she turned over, but she found it easy to drift into a lovely, restful haze.

Her security expert perched on a chair, head erect, eyes darting, drinking what he termed "sludge" coffee. Apparently he didn't realize her eyes remained open a slit. Was it yearning that crossed his face? A thread of longing wove its way into her dreams.

*   *   *

"Why am I always the last to know?" Hunter had repeated his concern for Shannon. Now he held her almost as gently as Beth had, sitting before her drawing room's fireplace. But his voice over her head cracked with frustration. "You could have been killed, but no one thought to call me."

"I'm sorry." Shannon stared into the undulating flames.

This is all about you? "Hopefully, there won't be a next time. But if so, I'll make sure you're at the top of the list." She reached up and ran her fingers along his cheek.

"I couldn't bear it if anything happened to you."

His hand tilted her chin up to look at him. His lips touched hers lightly, then pressed them with a sweetness and passion she couldn't deny.

Breathless, Shannon tried to think objectively. His kiss turned her inside out. However, maybe that kiss was only an act—part of his camouflage? Since the accident, Michael had patrolled the estate constantly. If he saw them through the window, would he view it that way?

Hunter snuggled her close to him, his teal sweater wafting subtle, spicy aftershave. Shannon focused on the gorgeous red roses he'd brought her and the way he absently turned the agate ring on his finger.

She drew back. "You're the most fascinating man I know. A scientist and an explorer! Maybe we can look for buried treasure together sometime." She laughed.

He didn't. "It gets a bit complicated."

"Have you sold your gold coin yet? I'd love to see—"

"Sorry. I sold it a few days ago to a collector from Southern California."

"Oh." Her disappointment was genuine. "Well, if you find a diamond-and-ruby necklace, I definitely want to see it."

He tweaked her nose. "I'll make sure you're at the top of the list."

*　　　*　　　*

"Good morning. Beth's Handy-Dandy Help, at your service."

Shannon looked up from the painting class schedules she'd been tweaking.

"No task too big or small. I do it all." Beth grinned from the doorway of Shannon's office. She held up a Pink Sprinkles bag with its black polka dots. "After a morning éclair break, of course."

"I'm all for the break." Shannon hugged her. "But Friday noon is one of your busiest days, right? Will you have time to drive back?"

"I decided I'd rather be here." Beth handed Shannon one of Joyce's delectable creations.

Even as they chatted and ate, Shannon added in her head the number of work days Beth had missed because of her, relegating Gourmet on the Go to her assistant. Although Tabitha was a wonderful cook, Shannon doubted she could mimic Beth's customer savvy, the TLC that made her business a success.

It's Beth's business, she reminded herself. *Not mine.* Shannon struggled with the work time she had lost. And more so, with her mother around constantly.

After break, she steered Beth to Essie, who welcomed her with open arms. "The stock room's calling your name."

In a single day, Beth transformed the room. Shannon had to admit her mother had accomplished the impossible task neither she nor Essie had time to tackle.

However, she'd brought her overnight bag too. That evening, Deborah cooked them her famous chicken and dumplings. They ate in the formal dining room, which looked a bit better after some repairs. Shannon enjoyed their time together as much as ever, but—

There it was. That big "but."

But Shannon wanted to study her grandfather's journal. With all that had been going on, she'd hardly touched it for a week.

The insurance process to repair her house and furnishings had proved incredibly complicated. After the numerous claims she'd made since moving into the mansion, she was shocked the company hadn't flat out dropped her when she informed them of her latest woes.

Between Hunter's smothering her, Michael's patrolling her every step, and her mother inviting herself over, Shannon wished she could jump on the next plane to Antarctica. Or Bongo Bongo. Anyplace she could spend an unmonitored evening alone.

Had she enjoyed quiet for one minute since the burglaries?

When she took James's logs to Captain Akiyama in Astoria, she'd felt carefree, exploring the Scandinavian shops, riding along the Riverwalk.

But not for long. She shuddered.

"Do you need a sweater?" Beth and Deborah chorused together.

"No." She fought an adolescent urge to roll her eyes.

Beth launched into a happy description of her Sweet Sixteen birthday party in this very room. Seeing her animated face, Shannon wondered again why Victoria hadn't left Beth the estate. She obviously loved it and considered it home. Why did Victoria leave it to Shannon instead—especially since her grandmother never once laid eyes on her?

Shannon surveyed the room with its newly repaired teakwood buffet, the enormous matching table, the elegant linens, china, and silver tea service—all of which she rarely used. The silver sconces on the walls. The dazzling crystal-and-bronze chandelier, in all its ornate glory.

Even as they bantered and told fun stories, a still, small voice whispered in Shannon's ear: *Did Beth ever wish it all belonged to her?*

— 16 —

The first time Shannon saw Witch Cave, scratching around in damp rock and earth had filled her with mounting exhilaration, even when she grew tired.

Now, with ribs and muscles griping at her, she wished she had listened to Michael and Deborah and stayed home.

But she wouldn't let Michael see a hint of that.

Taciturn after losing the argument, he offered no sympathy. He worked, casting only rare glances her way. Sometimes he grunted. She grunted back.

Scintillating conversation.

Shannon pushed a stray curl from her face with a muddy hand. Whatever had made her think digging for a treasure could be glamorous? The cave had morphed into a dank, nasty dungeon. Her grandfather had served a life sentence here. Shannon shook her head. No way would she do that. Surely, she, Michael, and the police would crack her burglary and assault cases before they dug up every inch of Smugglers' Cove.

She needed to explore that last clue—the "dark glass" one. In his journal, James had brushed it off. Angus, he said, liked taunting those who hunted his treasure. The old pirate couldn't resist a last gloat.

For Shannon, "dark glass" meant the shining black beads she either worked with or sold almost every day. Her geology professor had called it obsidian, often found in areas with a volcanic history—such as most of Oregon's coast. She groaned inwardly. *That's narrowing it down.*

But what did glass beads have to do with taunting treasure hunters? In frustration, Shannon gripped her head with gunky hands—then gave thanks she'd pulled a knit hat over her hair.

She let out a long breath and decided not to strain her gray matter. Not when she was this tired.

If only one of the Purls had joined them today! They could have brainstormed, talking and laughing to ease the hard hours along.

But she and Michael had planned to discuss new information he wanted to share. Info for her ear alone.

So discuss, she urged him. *Say something.*

She tried to catch his eye. He remained silent, a hulklike machine, bending, pushing, shoveling.

Shannon scooped out more muck, her arms growing heavier by the minute. Water welled up in the hole that she didn't bother to bail. She knelt and poked a thick metal skewer deep into the hole again and again, hoping that it might strike a wooden chest with a thud, clink against a metal hinge—something besides more mud and more rock.

Nothing.

"Tide's coming in. Ready to quit for the day?" he asked. Even in the shadows, she saw the same dirty stripes on his face that must have decorated hers.

And how. Shannon nodded.

He extended a hand, helped her up, and offered her his keys. "Want to warm up in the car? You'll find blankets in the backseat. I'll gather the tools."

His thoughtfulness left her nonplussed. She couldn't picture sitting in his Lexus, blanket or not. Even when she'd made mud pies as a child, she'd never achieved this level of sheer filthiness.

Fortunately, only a few visitors had parked cars in the beach lot, and she saw no one. Shivering in the ocean's chilly blast, Shannon brushed and scraped off as much of the muck as she could. She gingerly opened the door of Michael's beautiful car, thankful he'd brought several blankets. Shannon draped one on the black-and-silver leather front seat, swathed another around her, and edged into the car.

When Michael had picked her up, Shannon realized she hadn't ridden with him since their awful date. She'd spent hours then, trying to look perfect. Now she peered at herself in the rearview mirror and groaned.

Michael clunked the tools into the back, grabbed blankets, and joined her. He unscrewed a big silver thermos he'd brought. "I know you're mostly a tea drinker, but how does a cup of coffee sound?"

"Heavenly." The very aroma eased Shannon's aching body.

Michael poured it into large paper cups and handed her one. She returned his keys, and soon a delicious flow of air warmed her frostbitten toes. They basked in the heat, watching Wild Woman Waters live up to its name. Wave upon wave crashed against the rocks surrounding Witch Cave, swirling and leaping in a tempestuous dance. Shannon, sipping coffee, fought waves of contented drowsiness.

She noticed, though, that Michael didn't look as relaxed.

He cleared his throat. "I thought I'd brief you on my activities this week." His surveillance was a given. Michael popped up often at Espresso Yourself, gas stations, even the utility office where she paid her bills. "I tailed Hunter Banks on Tuesday."

The statement shouldn't have startled her. But it did. "And?"

For once, he didn't meet her gaze. "I followed him to Salem. He met an older, professorish guy at a restaurant. Looked like Banks was selling some artifacts. The man seemed more interested in a buckle and a piece of crockery Banks offered. But he also showed the guy a coin."

"Maybe *the* coin?" Shannon clasped her cup. "Oh, I wish he had let me see it!"

"I took pictures and enlarged them." Michael handed her a manila folder.

She inspected the amazingly detailed photos that showed the gold piece in Hunter's hand, with its handsome agate ring. In the hand of the prospective client. On the table. Scrutinizing all the photos, she cudgeled her brain to remember her research. Yes, it appeared to be a gold Spanish doubloon from the sixteenth century, featuring a coat of arms with a faintly outlined cross and a lion. Just as her grandfather had described in his journal.

She said quietly, "We can't prove it, but I'd be willing to bet this is the coin Grandfather hid in his secret room, the one that was to help lead the way to the treasure. I doubt it's a different coin from the one he tried to sell at the Butter Clam Inn. If he'd owned other coins besides Grandfather's, he could have offered to show me one when I asked. Instead, I think he lied about selling the original to a guy in California."

Michael nodded, but he still didn't meet her gaze.

You're right, OK? So what's this avoidance thing about?

"I agree that Hunter's involved in this, directly or indirectly," Shannon said. She cocked her head, trying to capture his eye. "Is there a problem with that?"

"Not at all." Finally he raised his chin. "But I found other evidence that he's been deceptive."

She couldn't read his expression. "Such as?"

"Banks teaches at Lawson College in Eureka, California, correct?"

"Yes." What was Michael getting at?

"You talked to him late at night when the second burglary occurred, right?"

"I did. He was in California then—"

"No, he wasn't."

Shannon stared. "Yes, he was."

"He *said* he was." Michael set his jaw. "You know Grayson suspects everybody, including Banks. Grayson called Banks's departmental office at the college."

"What did they say?"

"Hunter's not teaching this semester because of his research. But he often returns to his office in Eureka for a few days."

Though she'd already questioned Hunter's integrity, Shannon's stomach twisted.

Michael continued, "The head of the department confirmed Banks's presence in the office on the days the burglaries occurred. The secretary told the police the same story. According to her, he'd not only worked in his office the day of the second burglary, but a couple of days before. Banks's neighbors don't know him well, but they confirmed the house looked 'lived in.'"

"Sounds like he was in Eureka." Shannon tried to speak with conviction, but bile rose in her throat.

Michael shook his head. "I visited Lawson College a few days ago. I learned the department chairman hadn't actually seen Banks. He'd accepted the secretary's word that Banks had been in. Adjunct faculty, especially while doing research, pretty much come and go as they please."

Shannon wasn't quite sure how to respond, so she didn't.

"I invited the secretary out for Starbucks," Michael said. "Whitney Blake's the young, trusting type. When I informed her Banks might be involved in illegal activities, she broke down and told me he had talked her into lying about his days in Eureka. She took in his papers and mail, turned his lights on and off, parked her car in his driveway—even told other faculty members, including the chairman, that he'd been in and out."

"This secretary is young, trusting, and madly in love with him, I imagine?" Saying the words shouldn't have hurt, but they did.

Michael looked away.

No wonder Hunter had shown no signs of exhaustion on their ice-skating date. He hadn't driven seven hours from Eureka to Apple Grove. Shannon's churning stomach matched the waves that battered the shore. *He was probably holed up somewhere nearby, laughing at me.*

Michael broke the silence. "So what's your plan?"

She wanted to tell him to mind his own business. But she was his business. So was Hunter.

Shannon stared at her hands and planed the rage from her voice. "I'm not sure yet."

"When you do know, would you please keep me in the loop?" His clipped, professional tone.

In the loop? Part of her yelled, *How can you be so blasted objective? Why haven't you pounded Hunter into rubble?*

The sane part reminded her maybe she was just a job to Michael. He hadn't actually verbalized any feelings for her.

Shannon forced herself to look at his impassive face. "I'll let you know in a few days."

— 17 —

"Want to tell me more about the treasure clues?" Beth, knitting an orange blanket beside Shannon in her study, sounded like an eager third-grader. "Maybe we can brainstorm a little."

Actually, I don't want to. Shannon's last digging session at Witch Cave had put her to bed for a day. She still creaked and ached. Worse, Hunter was due in an hour and a half.

But Shannon bent, grimacing, and pulled James's journal from her bag beside the sofa. "I haven't felt much like exploring Smugglers' Cove lately."

"Of course you haven't. But we can work with the clues. And I'll help the Purls dig at the cave on Saturday." Beth's eyes glinted like green glass. "The sooner we solve this, the sooner we'll find the slime who ran you down."

Or the sooner we'll find the treasure? The unbidden notion had niggled her several times since she'd come home from the hospital. Beth, who barely tolerated the mention of her father's quest, now seemed obsessed by it. Shannon hoped this enthusiasm stemmed from motherly concern—not an expectation of a financial bailout. Not like Victoria's other greedy relatives.

Hating herself for such thoughts, Shannon handed her mother the journal and the magnifying glass.

Beth passed it over James's writing, squinting. "Sometime, you'll have to take me to Sidhe Glen. You knew the *sidhe* are faeries, right?"

Shannon nodded. "I expected the glen to be odd, even ghoulish."

Beth chuckled wryly. "Correct. Scottish faeries are no relation to Tinkerbell."

"Instead, it's grand and beautiful. No wonder the Salish tribes hold it sacred." Shannon sighed. "We haven't found Black Donald's Hand yet. Or Parable Rock. Possibilities, but nothing concrete because of all the earthquakes since Angus's era."

She took the journal from her mother, turned the page, and pointed at the sketch of the map. "Witch Cave and Wild Woman Waters fit this and Grandfather's descriptions so well. Otherwise, I might think I made a mistake about the treasure's location." Shannon chewed her lip. "Sometimes I'm not sure this is worth it."

Beth's eyes widened. "You hardly want to give up at this stage."

You don't either, do you? Shannon's suspicions yammered. *Give up a fabulous fortune? Never.* She dropped her head into her hand and tried to press such thoughts into nothing.

"Don't be discouraged," Beth soothed her. "You're tired and hurting. Things will look up."

"Perhaps. But," Shannon lifted her hands, then let them drop, "I know most of Angus's descendants didn't come to Oregon, but a few did, and they never found the treasure. Grandfather had the map, and he never found it. Why do I think I have even a miniscule chance?"

"Because your brilliant mother is helping you. Next clue."

Shannon couldn't help laughing. "How could I forget?" She glanced at her list again. "Dark glass ... I thought it might have something to do with obsidian."

"I used to find bits of it on the beach," Beth said, knitting

again, but her expression told Shannon she'd wandered back
to an earlier time.

"Another unspecific clue. Probably affected by the
earthquakes as well." Shannon shook her head. "Tomorrow
I'll call Aaron. Maybe he can tell me whether obsidian is
found in large concentrations around Smugglers' Cove."
She frowned. "But it may have nothing to do with geology.
Grandfather thought the 'dark glass' implied Angus was
jeering at those who sought his treasure." She plopped a
fist into a nearby pillow. "I wish I could read the entire clue!
There must be much more to it than 'dark glass.'"

"Strange," Beth agreed. "But then, Father hated to lose.
Not finding the treasure probably enraged him. Perhaps he
wrote that bit when he'd had a drop too much. Or maybe ...."

"Maybe what?" Shannon stared at her mother's odd
expression.

Beth half-chuckled. "Angus did not follow the Bible,
but like many of his era, he was biblically literate. Perhaps
he was referring to a scripture in which St. Paul said we 'see
through a glass darkly.' Maybe the glass is a mirror."

"Well, that certainly clears up everything," Shannon
chortled. "An ancestor's egotism, obsidian, a Bible verse,
and a mirror." Laughing felt good. She shouldn't let her
troubles weigh her down. "Here's another weird word Kate
found in one of James's logs. I spotted it in the journal
too, when I used the magnifying glass. James wrote briefly
about his family line, that his granddad told him Angus's
wife was a Soaper—"

"What?" The color drained from Beth's face. "What did
you say?"

"Soaper." Shannon leaned forward. Her mother looked ghastly. "Are you all right? Can I fetch you a glass of water?"

Beth's knitting dropped to the floor. She fell back into her chair and murmured, "I hoped I would never hear that word again."

"I'm so sorry." How could some laundry-like term throw her mother into such a panic?

"It's all right. You didn't know." Beth's chilly hand, still trembling, patted Shannon's.

"Know what?" Shannon tried to rub warmth back into her mother's fingers.

Beth inhaled a shaky breath and whispered, "Long ago, in Scotland, I heard that word. When one of the Camorra kidnapped me."

Shannon sucked in a breath and held it.

Beth went on: "She blindfolded me, dragged me to a house, and whispered 'Soaper' as a password at the door. They ripped the tape off my mouth. Both the woman and her accomplice lit cigarettes and—and—questioned me."

Shannon said, "I knew you loathed cigarette smoke, but I didn't know why." *I didn't know why little round scars dotted your arms, either.*

Beth closed her eyes. "They must have grown confident of their remote hiding place, because soon my kidnapper fairly shouted 'Soaper!' each day when she arrived to question me again."

Shannon gathered her trembling mother in her arms. "They can't hurt you anymore, Beth."

Slowly the shaking ceased. "I'm sorry." Beth shook her head. "After thirty-five years, I shouldn't let bad memories do that to me."

Shannon stroked her hair. "The miracle is that you're still sane."

"Somewhat, anyway." A tiny smile released Beth's taut face for a moment, then vanished.

Shannon said, "We don't have to talk about this anymore."

"I think we do." Her mother sounded very motherlike. "I assume you're unfamiliar with the obscure Scottish legend involved?"

"I'd never heard of the Soapers until Kate and I read it in Grandfather's stuff."

"I hadn't either until I investigated the Camorra," Beth said. "The Soapers represented the worst of the *sidhe*. They were half-human, half-faerie creatures who lived near water in remote areas. They often disguised themselves as harmless women who offered food, shelter, and laundry services to weary travelers. Instead, they washed the wanderers' cloaks in their own blood."

"How awful!" The firelight in Shannon's cozy study seemed to dim with the story.

Beth continued, "The legend wasn't commonly shared, because the story shamed the clans involved. While supernatural aspects were mythological, the evil women were not. Down through the centuries, Soaper-like women have appeared in our ancestral lines." Her face grew grim. "Both sides of my family—the honorable Paisleys and the Shaws— tried to forget their ties to the Soapers."

"*Both* sides?"

"Like many Scottish clans, they were interrelated."

A lovely double legacy. Shannon gulped, but she had to know. "So when you investigated the Camorra, you met up with Soapers?"

Beth nodded. "Those women in my clans who pledged loyalty to the Camorra adopted the Soaper persona as a sort of mascot. They all used it as a password." Beth almost spat the words.

Fierce red patches blotched her mother's gray cheeks. Had the emotional strain shot Beth's blood pressure through the roof?

Shannon slipped an arm around her. "But they no longer wield the power they used to—partly because your research eventually led to the Camorra's exposure. You know that."

"I know." Beth sagged against Shannon for a moment, then straightened. "I'm hoping the treasure clues involve the Soapers in name only. But the very mention of their name …."

"I can understand your reaction." Shannon soothed her, yet she turned cold, revolted by the evil associated with this one clue. "This makes me even more thankful that the state will lay claim to anything we find." She picked up her knitting. "Right now, I don't want to touch the treasure with a ten-foot— a hundred-foot!—needle."

"I'm glad." The goofy comment brought a hint of a smile to Beth's face. She resumed her row on the blanket. "I hate, *hate* all this, but perhaps it will end the shadow that stupid treasure has cast on our family all these years."

"If it does, it will be worth it." Shannon added a few more rows to her sock. "Maybe then we can sit around the fire on cold nights gossiping about the twins instead of macabre ancestors and creepy clues."

"Certainly works for me." Beth nestled into the sofa. She cocked her head at Shannon. "But as for sitting around the fire all evening—don't you have a date tonight?"

Shannon stopped knitting and dropped her head in her hands. "Yes. I totally forgot."

"She said with a distinct lack of delight," Beth mused as her keen eyes searched Shannon's face.

"I'm still not sure what Hunter's about." She hadn't told Beth about the fake phone call from California. "I need to find out."

"I know." Beth wielded one needle like a dagger. "If you didn't, I'd scare him off for you."

"No thanks." Deborah and her loaded .22 spooked Shannon enough. "But I would appreciate it if you'd keep your cell on. We're going to the Terrace Steakhouse in Wellington. If things get complicated—"

"Do you want me to follow you—wait in the parking lot?"

"That's not necessary. It's only fifteen or so miles away." What if Beth charged in at the exact moment she'd backed Hunter into a corner? Shannon wanted to handle things her way. "I'd better lock the journal in the vault-room for the night."

She hurried to the back stairs closet and took care of business before pausing in front of the mirror in the foyer. She brushed glitter and lint off the sage green sweater she'd worn to work and glanced at her hair as Beth appeared. "Not stellar, but do I pass?"

"You're beautiful. He doesn't deserve you." Beth grimaced as the front doorbell chimed. "That's probably Mr. Wonderful now."

"I'll see you later." Shannon hugged her mother goodbye. She didn't say "Don't wait up," because she knew Beth would anyway. Deborah too.

Hunter presented her with more roses—peach-hued this time. "You look gorgeous. I don't deserve such beauty."

Shannon blinked at his following of Beth's script. "Thank you."

"Hello, Hunter." Her mother stayed at Shannon's elbow.

"Evening, Ms. Jacobs." Hunter raised the charm factor a notch and steered Shannon toward the door.

"Now, don't bring her home late," Beth joked, but the glint in her eyes did not match her nice-lady smile.

Shannon smothered a chuckle, watching Hunter fidget under her mother's eye. But Beth needn't worry.

Given her plans for the evening, Hunter would bring her home soon enough.

18

"**I** didn't know your mother was staying with you tonight."

Hunter's disappointment made Shannon doubly glad for Beth's presence. "I didn't either. She drops in now and then."

On the way to the restaurant, Shannon drew Hunter into a conversation about his co-workers. After they'd ordered, he entertained her with fun, often satirical stories about fellow professors. They finished their dinner with what she guessed was an excellent imitation of his department head.

They both were laughing when she dropped her bomb: "But what about Whitney Blake? You haven't mentioned her this evening."

Long pause. Hunter, freeze-dried smile still intact, said, "You've met her?"

"Maybe." Shannon's smile disappeared. "I know a lot about her."

Hunter's shoulders drooped. The smile morphed into his little-boy look. "She's just a cute kid, Shannon. She doesn't mean anything to me."

"I can believe that." Shannon raised her chin. "Why was it so important that she lie for you? That you make me believe you were in California rather than Apple Grove?"

"It wasn't like that—"

"Then enlighten me." She crossed her arms. "Tell me the truth—if you can, Hunter."

For the first time, he met her gaze. "More is going on than you know, Shannon. Far more than I can discuss in public. Your mother's back at your house, so we can't have privacy there. Let's go to my apartment."

Shannon arched an eyebrow.

Hunter raised a hand. "This isn't a come-on, I promise! I'll explain everything. Over a chai so good you won't believe it."

The unwavering look-you-in-the-face appeal. The pleading note in his voice.

The way he fingered his agate ring—which he'd done every time he'd lied to her.

"All right." Shannon funneled hurt and hope into her words as she rose. She gestured toward the restroom sign in the back. "I'll meet you in the foyer in a few minutes."

She sauntered through the dining room. Upon pushing open the restroom door, however, she paused. The usual weekend line of women strung along the wall. So much for privacy. She exited and found a niche a pay phone had once occupied. Huddled against the wall, she called Beth.

"Can you pick me up? Hunter's up to something. I'll wait inside the fence around the restaurant dumpster." She'd already noted a back exit she could use.

"I'm on it." Beth didn't ask questions. Shannon hung up.

Cold metal poked Shannon's back through her sweater. An arm snaked around her waist.

"Please don't scream." Hunter's still-polite tone turned her stomach.

"What are you doing?"

"Turn the phone off. Pretend you're sick, and everything will be fine."

Shannon didn't have to pretend. Hunter flung her coat around her and pulled her close. She wanted to gag, but she let him edge her down the hallway where employees, concern crossing their faces, asked if they could help.

"I'm taking her to the emergency room." Hunter played the part of the concerned boyfriend perfectly. The gun jabbed her as he guided them out the rear exit into the night, where the chilly November wind ravaged her face.

"If only you'd backed off a little," he muttered.

Did she detect a note of pain in his voice? Shannon flung back, "If you think this will help you find the treasure, you're out of your mind."

"Oh, I'll find it."

She'd never seen him set his jaw like this, his lips pulled back from whitened teeth. Still, he didn't shove her into his SUV, just opened the door with his usual gentlemanly demeanor and helped her in, all the while training his revolver on her.

Hunter whipped two lengths of rope from his pocket and tied her hands and feet.

"Came prepared, didn't you?" Shannon glared at him. "Did you learn those knots in Boy Scouts?"

He shot her a deadly look. "Don't try anything. You can't open this door after I close it."

Nausea nearly drowned her. *Beth, please come. Please.*

If only she'd accepted her mother's offer to wait in the parking lot.

Hunter entered the driver's side, then pulled her phone from her bag. He laughed mirthlessly. "You won't need this."

Stall him. "Was all this part of Li Chung's plan too?"

Hunter started, then cloaked his tone with normalcy.

"How I find the treasure makes no difference to him. More than the gold, he wants a pearl brooch."

"A brooch?" She stared.

"Some family heirloom."

"But you want the treasure." Shannon dug at him. "So you're both planning to play nice and share?"

Hunter started the SUV with a roar. He flung it into reverse, but navigated the parking lot at normal speed.

Shannon gritted her teeth. If he'd peeled out, some cranky onlooker might have noticed. She cast desperate looks around the lot. Did restaurants use video surveillance?

Already, Hunter had turned onto roads she didn't know. She obeyed her investigative instincts and memorized landmarks, but the quivering in her stomach spread to her knees, her hands, her lips.

Why didn't he stop and blindfold her?

Because you won't live long enough to tell anyone where you've been.

Tears trembled in her eyes as the car whizzed past a few remaining convenience stores, deeper and deeper into coastal forests. She tried not to recall the banter they'd shared while riding together.

Get him talking. Maybe if she could revive some fragment of their camaraderie, he wouldn't sink to subhuman levels. "Are we taking another surprise trip to the beach? Like we did on my birthday?"

Hunter flinched as if she'd turned the revolver on him.

"We had a lot of fun." She infused sadness into her tone. "I liked your surprises. Much more than this one."

He didn't unbolt his gaze from the road, but that hint

of regret colored his words again. "We could have had more together, Shannon. If only you'd kept out of it—"

"I was supposed to ignore two burglaries?" Her anger boiled over. "I shouldn't be concerned when some goon runs over me and leaves me for dead?"

"I didn't know Chung was going to do that." Hunter's voice cracked.

"But you knew about the burglaries he planned. In fact, you carried them out for him." Shannon hurled the words at him. "You'd been in my house. You knew Deborah often forgot to activate the security system. You only had to wait for the perfect opportunity, and then you took my grandfather's map and coin from his desk. You've been playing me for a fool all along!"

"Shannon, I didn't enjoy any of this—"

"Really? Whoever tore my house apart appeared to love destroying beautiful things. Why did you do that?"

Hunter hunched over the wheel. "You had something that guided you to Smugglers' Cove. We weren't sure what it was then, but we had to find it."

"So you *did* follow me." She shot the words like bullets. "You did all this for Li Chung?"

He stared straight ahead. "He's my boss."

No wonder Hunter never lacked for "grant money." "So you'd do anything for him. For the treasure, right?"

He glared at her, eyes blazing green fire. "It's not just the money. It's a matter of justice."

Justice? She gagged. Trussed like a Thanksgiving turkey, her ribs still hurt from a near-fatal "accident," and he mouthed the word *justice?*

"You have no idea who I am, do you?" His righteous anger faded to a superior smile.

"You tell me." Shannon implanted a tiny barb in each word.

"I'll give you a hint. My middle name starts with a C."

Charles? Charlemagne? Chimichanga? "I'm not in the mood for guessing games, Hunter."

"Neither am I, lovely lady." The last words sounded like a snarl.

She'd better watch her mouth. Her heart raced like an approaching train.

"My middle name is Cornelius. After my grandfather." He floored the accelerator, barely making a curve in the winding road.

Cornelius.

Corny.

James and Corny had sought the treasure together.

Hunter took the next curve at a more bearable speed. "I see you're beginning to understand."

She hesitated to trigger his anger again, but she had to know. "Yes … but I don't know the details."

"I'll tell you details." The speedometer climbed again. "Your grandfather promised my grandfather they would get rich together. Captain Paisley dangled the treasure in front of Grandpa's nose while he did most of the dirty work. Grandpa was sent to the Pacific during World War II." Hunter's lip curled. "Paisley must have breathed a sigh of relief when my grandfather was killed in action. Now Paisley would have the treasure all to himself."

Shannon bit her lip. Grandfather hadn't gloated when Corny died. Did she dare say it?

"Grandpa left a very young girlfriend with a baby boy. Grandma thought Captain Paisley would help her when he returned from the war, a noble hero." Hunter laughed, a sound that reminded Shannon of nails pulled from old wood. "Instead, he refused to talk to her. Grandma and her baby—my father—nearly starved."

Surely not. Grandfather, despite his faults, had a heart. Shannon was sure of it. But she didn't contradict Hunter. Eyes lit like flashlights, he laid rubber with every twist of the road.

Hunter continued: "My dad never got a break, growing up. Neither did I." He glared at her. "Do you know how many toilets I cleaned to graduate from college?"

She'd worked to help finance her schooling too. But he didn't wait to hear it.

"Dad drank himself to death. But not before I promised him I'd find the treasure."

At his bitter words, a thread of compassion wove itself through Shannon's terror. Hunter was doing wrong. But he'd suffered from his family's choices. Oh, she understood that. "I would have shared the money with you, Hunter."

He gripped the steering wheel as if he wanted to yank it out.

She said softly, "But it's not mine to share. I'm sure you know about Oregon's antiquities laws."

"Written by rich legislators." He scoffed. "Passed by people who never cleaned a john in their lives."

Somehow, she had to get through to him. Before they arrived at their destination. Shannon barely smothered a scream as they took a curve on two wheels. *Or before his driving kills us both.*

"You don't have to do this, Hunter. You don't have to ruin your life—"

"Spare me." He pulled out his revolver and cocked the hammer. "Tell me where the journal is. Tell me."

"Tell me where the map is," Shannon replied, tossing her head. "And the doubloon you *didn't* sell."

In answer, he let the hammer down, stuck the revolver in a cup holder and plunged the SUV onto a gravel road almost as twisted as he was. The car hopped like a rabbit on steroids. Her bruised side slammed against the door with every bump.

"How did you find out about the journal?" Shannon edged her bound hands toward the revolver, inch by inch.

"Bank tellers have their price too." He glanced sideways. "No you don't."

He stuck the gun into his pocket again.

Amazing how his smirk still held a dark shadow of little-boy appeal.

A poisonous despair flooded through her. If only Michael knew where she was ....

He'd arrested drug dealers with nice smiles.

This kidnapper's sweet grin probably surpassed them all.

— 19 —

"Tell me where the journal is, Shannon." Hunter pointed the revolver at her again.

The gravel road had ended less than a quarter mile from Dawson Beach. Hunter had untied Shannon, forcing her to the shoreline where the pounding surf nearly drowned out his words. Few people came here, even during good weather, because of dangerous undertows and a deadly seawall of rocks that smashed boats and daredevil surfers. Now the wind-driven mist from each wave's crash soaked Shannon's leather boots. Her aches protested at the water's chill, the air's dankness. She faced Hunter, her back to the ocean that roared and clawed at her. She said nothing.

"Shannon." That tinge of sorrow sounded in his voice again. "I know you've been hiding it in multiple places. Tell me now. I don't want to do this."

Poor baby. "You really expect me to hand it over? When that's the only thing keeping me alive?"

"Li Chung just wants the brooch—"

"He probably doesn't want to go to prison. Neither do you." She fought the despondency that wrapped dark, tight wings around her. "I know far too much. You'll get rid of me, whether I tell you or not."

"That's not true." Panic eroded Hunter's voice. "After we find the treasure, Chung said I could take you abroad—"

"You believed him?" She laughed bitterly. He thought she'd party with him on some tropical island? Shannon slathered her words with acid. "That sounds fun, though. We'd have such a good time."

Tattered shreds of moonlight clung to his face. "Tell me where the journal is. Or—or you'll have to walk into the sea." His voice broke.

You can't bring yourself to shoot me, can you? Was he even giving her a chance to escape?

The monster sea howled in derision. Hypothermia, undertows, waves taller than Shannon, rocky teeth that could chew her up ....

Some chance.

She realized, too, that drowning might prove quite tidy— no direct evidence that she'd been murdered. No weapons or ballistic evidence. Rescuers might search for days before they found her body. If they found it at all.

Even so, she'd rather take her chances with the killer surf than Hunter's gun. She didn't think he would shoot. But given the past few weeks, she wouldn't bet her life on it.

"Walk, Shannon." He gestured with the gun again. "Tell or walk."

He resembled a scarecrow, the wind yanking at his hair and coat. Shannon turned and took several steps, the water snatching at her with demonic glee.

Deeper. Deeper.

A breaker battered her, nearly knocking her off her feet. *God, it's me again. Help.*

Should she talk? Turn around and say, "The journal's in my secret room. If you ask Deborah nicely, she'll hand it right over."

"Shannon, stop!"

Beth?

Her mother shouted again, "Come back! I've got things under control."

What? How? Shannon turned. Hunter no longer pointed the gun at her.

Numb feet and legs. Could she walk on them? Shannon shoved her feet forward as if they were anchors. Left. Right. Left-right-left-right, and then she ran, the deprived waves licking at her. Warm tears spurted down Shannon's cheeks, mixing with icy saltwater. She stumbled onto the gravelly beach, wanting to throw her arms around Beth.

But Beth's mother-bear eyes were fixed on Hunter, and she held a butcher knife to his back. "Don't move, you scum."

Her deadly tone belied her pastel raincoat and mom jeans.

Hunter didn't move. But he talked. "I wouldn't have let you drown, Shannon. You have to believe me—"

"Actually, I don't." Her deadened lips muffled the words, but they were worth the effort.

Beth ordered Hunter, "Toss her your coat. But don't try anything. I have a knack with knives, and I would love to julienne you into a garnish."

He obeyed. Shannon flinched at the smell of Hunter's aftershave in the parka, but swathed in its comforting warmth, she could live with it. Especially as sleet attacked his clothes, his hair, his face.

"How did you find me?" Shannon quavered.

Her mother still didn't take her eyes off Hunter. "I pulled into the restaurant parking lot as he pulled out, and I followed his car. A challenge, but I've tailed maniacs before."

She gestured with her head. "Shannon, would you please pick up his gun?"

Shannon bent down and reached.

A female stranger's toxic voice said, "Touch it, and you're dead."

*   *   *

"Idiot." A lovely, red-nailed hand slapped Hunter so hard he swayed. "I knew I couldn't trust you to do anything right. What Chung sees in you, I'll never know."

The Asian woman from the Butter Clam Inn and Chung's downtown building.

Clutching some sort of automatic rifle.

An armed henchman grabbed Beth's knife. Another scooped up Hunter's gun and threw him against the rock wall. Both were Asian, and for an absurd moment, Shannon wondered if she'd stumbled onto a Jackie Chan movie set.

The shove that the woman gave her, however, felt very real. "Did you really think I didn't know you followed me?" Her perfect scarlet lip curled. "Too bad you couldn't take a hint. You had to come back for more, didn't you?"

Standing beside Shannon, Beth radiated rage like fallout. Shannon raised an eyebrow at her mother. She herself would love to rip this woman's dangly gold earrings from her lobes, but above all, they had to keep their heads.

"Put them in the van," the woman snarled. "We'll go to Chung's cottage and see what he wants to do."

Their captors bound and blindfolded them, tossing them into the back of a blue van. Listening to breathing next to her, Shannon recoiled. Hunter. His arm touched her. His fingers clasped hers. She balled them into a fist.

"Don't let Bai scare you," he whispered. "I'll work it out with Chung."

She tried to scoot away. *You're certainly in a position to negotiate, aren't you?*

A growl erupted from the guard in the front seat. He ripped a bandanna to shreds and climbed into the back. He jammed a piece into Hunter's mouth, then one into Shannon's. The coarse, greasy cloth made her retch. *Thanks, Hunter.* While she didn't mind that her ex-boyfriend had been silenced, she winced at her mother's moan.

Another eternity of bone-bruising bumps. Only now, the van's hot metal floor slammed against Shannon's bare cheek.

Was Beth all right? Shannon shifted her rope-bound ankles and carefully probed with her feet.

Something wiggled her toe. Beth was conscious. Gladness touched Shannon, like a sip of water in the Sahara. *Oh, God, my mother has endured enough. Somehow, some way, help us escape.*

Shannon fought to stay awake, to listen for clues as to their direction and destination. She soon suspected their captors were camouflaging their route to fool not only their unwilling passengers but the police as well. Endless winding roads tangled her sense of direction. Little conversation went on in the front seat. Nothing that told her where they were going. Their driver didn't listen to the radio, which might have helped Shannon approximate their locations. Only a series of wailing country songs from his iPod—she classified that as part of the torture. Eventually she shut down, too choked with pain and weariness to remain alert.

Finally, a wrenching stop, and the squeaky rear doors swung open. Chilly air rushed into the van, sharp as fear and salty, carrying the rhythm of the sea. Though Shannon wondered if she would have to walk into the sea again, she welcomed the change from the nauseating odor of gasoline and Hunter's aftershave.

Rough hands dragged her and the others from the van and dumped them onto the ground. Someone untied her ankles and yanked her onto her numb feet. Shannon fell over like a redwood.

Chinese words, but she understood their fury. A large, hairy being lifted her and threw her over his brawny shoulder. He carried her inside, away from the fresh air, from the boundless pulse of the ocean. She couldn't see her mother, but a razor-edged ribbon of agony stretched between them.

Don't worry.

I'll be OK.

Her telepathy translated into little real assurance, but she sent it just the same.

Shannon's captor threw her onto a tiled floor, squatted beside her and pulled the gag from her mouth. A powerful hand seized her chin, groped down her neck, her sweater—

Chinese words again. Bai used them like rapiers. The hand released her.

Someone flicked a light switch, and a door closed. Shannon still wore a blindfold, but she sensed every vestige of light had gone from the room.

She wondered if she would live to see it return.

20

"Where am I?" Shannon demanded.

Her own voice startled her. She didn't know how long she had lain, silent and blind, in the dark. When her burly guard removed the blindfold, she'd rejoiced, but now the look he gave her shriveled her insides.

Was he the one who had terrorized her upon arrival? If he was, he hadn't tried anything since.

She commanded her brain to recall the trip to this place, but darkness clogged her memory to only a trickle.

Hunter. She'd rather forget him.

Bumpy, twisty roads. At the end of their journey, she'd sensed ocean air and sounds after careless hands yanked her from a van.

Arrival where? Shannon hadn't a clue.

The guard showed her a shower stall. He brought her a bare-bones grooming kit and a towel, untying her.

Why? Kidnappers generally didn't care about hygiene.

No lock on the bathroom door.

Shannon trembled.

Though her sore body craved a hot shower, she could not bear the thought of him hovering outside.

If he stayed outside.

Nevertheless, if she was going to die, she might as well die clean. Shannon broke her five-minute college shower record, especially when she discovered the hot water hardly deserved the H on the old-fashioned faucet.

Despite terror that chilled her almost as much as the water, Shannon marveled at how a woman could face anything, as long as she'd washed her hair. Yesterday's clothes didn't feel so grubby.

She could even face her gargantuan captor. When his eyes electrified at the sight of her, she studied the clean but ugly brown-flecked floor tile.

He marched her down a different hallway. A natal longing for her mother had gripped her. Now the hunger squeezed her stomach even more than lack of food. Would she see Beth? Was her mother still alive?

They climbed utilitarian steps to a door he unbolted, then unlocked with an elaborate keypad code.

Shannon gasped.

Lilting music from a bronze dragon fountain greeted her. Small palms graced it, with a backdrop of two huge purple silk fans painted with dragons and Chinese characters.

Shannon didn't realize she had paused until the guard pushed her. She waded through the dense carpets. Sandalwood and clove incense clouded the air, stinging her eyes as they walked past brilliant tapestries. Each turn took Shannon deeper and deeper into an exotic Oriental world. Chung's world.

A world with no windows. At least, she hadn't seen any.

Adrenaline pumped through her veins. Shannon prayed with every step.

The guard opened French doors into a dining room more beautiful than the hall. Ceiling-high black carved screens filtered light from many windows onto red walls and bronze mirrors. A black lacquered table edged with gold dragons stretched from one end of the room to the other, bountiful with porcelain dishes of steaming food.

The gorgeous room contrasted with Shannon's not-so-fresh clothes. Her stomach growled like a starved tiger. How long had it been since the steak dinner with Hunter before he had abducted her?

A small, gray-haired man wearing a dark sweater and slacks sat in a chair too big for him. To Shannon's surprise, he rose and bowed before her, speaking with slightly accented English. "I am Li Chung. Please sit."

What if I don't?

She would accomplish nothing by antagonizing him. Shannon sat.

Chung spoke in Chinese to the guard, who left. Servants materialized like genies, bringing Shannon the most delicious foreign foods she'd ever tasted. Who knew when she would eat again? She'd read accounts of Asian jailers treating prisoners with extreme courtesy, then extreme cruelty to further disorient them. So she chewed slowly, hoping her jittery stomach wouldn't overreact.

At meal's end, a servant brought exquisite bowls of tea and stood beside the French doors, motionless. Shannon sipped.

"You have a family?"

He spoke in a grandfatherly tone.

"Yes." No doubt, Chung already knew about those close to her. But Shannon answered, "I'm a widow. I have two grown children. You may have met my mother."

"Ah, yes. Beth Jacobs." He leaned forward, small hands

clasped on the table. "We have that in common. Our families are important to us."

She raised her eyes and looked into his smooth, ageless face, with its olive-pit eyes behind silver glasses.

He signaled the servant to refill the tea. "I want the treasure for family reasons."

So you resort to burglary? Kidnapping?

"The gold interests me, of course, but my primary focus is a one-of-a-kind golden brooch in the shape of a monkey. Its unique pearl was considered the finest in existence. My family cherished it as its prize jewel for hundreds of years." His mild voice hardened. "Until merchants from the Philippines, under the guise of traders, stole it from my ancestors."

"I did not know that." What else could she say?

He continued as if she hadn't spoken. "The merchants sold the brooch to the Spanish. The English pirate, Sir Frances Drake, evidently stole it from the Spanish. And your ancestor, Angus Paisley, stole it from his captain." A wry smile tugged at Chung's mouth. "An interesting tableau. Pirates stealing from pirates."

"I have stolen nothing." Shannon kept her tone neutral. "I don't intend to steal the treasure—the gold, the brooch, or anything else."

"I know." The same gentle tone. "But you would hand it over to the state. That must not happen."

Shannon raised her chin. "I knew nothing about the treasure and would not have pursued it, had you not forced the issue by burglarizing my home."

"I understand." Chung spoke as if discussing an error in an insurance policy. "Unfortunate that you became involved.

Nevertheless, the brooch must be restored to my family. We are the rightful owners." He touched her arm with cold, dry fingers. "Tell me all you know about the treasure. All. Leave nothing out."

As if Chung had signaled, Bai, dressed in a black business suit, entered and sat beside Shannon. She did not drink tea.

"If you had approached me in an *honorable* way"—Shannon noted the tightening of Chung's jaw—"I would have offered what help I could. Obviously, you have resources at your disposal that I lack." *Like henchmen. And world-class tech criminals.* She cleared her throat. "But I will share what I know, which isn't much, since I don't have the map."

Chung knew about the journal, of course, but she wouldn't add that information until she had to. Instead, she related what she knew about the Simmuem River, Black Donald's Hand, and Sidhe Glen. She said nothing about Witch Cave.

Her listeners sat like statues. Shannon tried to pretend they were. She detected no reaction, no communication between Bai and Chung. But at the end of her recital, Bai raised her delicate eyebrows at the servant, who opened the French doors.

Shannon repressed a gasp as the burly guard shoved Beth into the room so hard that she sprawled on the floor. Shannon jumped to help her, but Bai's long fingernails bolted Shannon's arm to the table.

Beth's red hair matted in clumps. Her clothing looked dirty and torn. Shannon stared in horror at her mother's glassy eyes, the bruises that marred her face.

"You have not told us the whole truth." Chung didn't change expression. He gestured toward Beth. "How important is your family to you?"

Clean and well fed, Shannon roiled with guilt. She longed to smash the man's statue face.

"Where is the journal?" He ground the words between his teeth.

Beth shook her head at Shannon. Bai rose. Her hand whipped across Beth's face.

Shannon bit her lip so hard she tasted blood. She ached to spew out information about the journal, about Angus, the Soapers—but neither she nor Beth would live long if she divulged all.

Bai slipped a gold-handled knife from a sheath under her jacket. She dragged Shannon from her chair and backed her against the wall. Bai angled the blunt edge of the knife into Shannon's windpipe and pressed hard.

Harder.

We're both going to die. Nobody knows where we are—

Bai stroked the razor edge lightly across Shannon's throat. A hot stripe of pain blazed across her neck. "Shall I do this to your children?"

"I know where the treasure is." Beth struggled to stand. "But I'll tell you nothing unless you let Shannon go."

"She doesn't know anything!" Shannon shouted desperately. With a lightning movement, Bai slammed Shannon's head against the wall. She dropped to the carpet, stained by scarlet drops of her blood. Her vision blurred, and she shut her eyes.

"Enough." Chung's voice sounded disapproving. Big hands yanked Shannon to her feet and dropped her into a chair. Pain detonated in her head. When she forced her eyes open, a blurry Chung, silver glasses shining, still sat in his big chair. "Tell me what else you know. Now. Or I promise you and your family will die. Quite slowly. Very painfully."

"The journal ..." Where was it? Nausea swirled inside her. Pictures of the secret room floated in her mind. A man's face with blue, blue eyes. She couldn't think of his name. "Rock. Soap ...."

Bai raised her hand again.

Beth yelled, "She can't tell you where the treasure is. I can."

"No!" Shannon screamed. "Beth ... knows ... nothing!"

Chung dragged Shannon from her chair, his small hands like vises. He shoved her toward the burly guard. "Kill her. Any way you choose. Let me know when it is done."

The man's yellow-toothed mouth curved in a bear's grin. His hands gripped her as if he would break her in two.

Oh, God. Help.

A deafening blast shook the room. Screams. His hands clenched her close to his monster body as they both fell.

"Don't move."

Michael?

He loomed over them, his lips drawn in a snarl. He'd dug a shotgun muzzle into her captor's chest.

Shannon wanted to leap, to dance, to plant a kiss on Michael that would last a week.

But her muscles were spaghetti. Her wobbly lips couldn't form words.

An EMT rushed to her side and examined her bloody throat. "Looks like a flesh wound, though I'm sure it hurts like crazy." He taped gauze to her neck and confirmed Shannon could see and move her extremities, though feebly. "I'll return in a sec, ma'am. Have to help with some others."

Shannon fumbled "B-Beth?" to his retreating back.

"The EMTs will take good care of her." Michael gestured to an officer, who dug his own weapon into the guard's chest. Michael crouched beside her. "How are you feeling? I suppose you're 'fine'?"

His gun-metal eyes softened to blue. A callused finger touched her cheek.

Tears dammed deep inside her now flowed freely.

The other officer prodded the guard to his feet. Shannon averted her eyes, noticing for the first time the other police handcuffing an expressionless Chung, an expletive-breathing Bai, and their henchmen. Drifting patches of white smoke filled the room. Shannon coughed.

Michael answered her unspoken question. "We used a flash-bang to surprise them. Doesn't blow things up like a normal grenade. Just creates enough noise and light to distract perps for a few seconds."

She only half-listened, because she was watching the EMTs raise a gurney with her mother on it. Beth's small frame lay still, her eyes closed, face gray and bruise-purple against the white sheet. A blue-uniformed woman wearing a stethoscope dropped beside Shannon.

"Will Beth be all right?" Shannon struggled to sit up.

Michael and the attendant restrained her. "You'd be wise to stay put until I check you out," the attendant said.

"I'm her daughter." Shannon lay back, but she had to know. "Please tell me."

"We didn't find broken bones, but she's experiencing significant pain. Her vitals are strong, though she's dehydrated and may need an IV." The cheerful blonde patted Shannon's arm gently. "We'll take her to the hospital—"

"No hospital," Beth said from the gurney, her eyes still closed.

"You'll stay there if I have to chain you," Shannon retorted.

"Fine. We'll share a room." Beth opened her eyes and shot Shannon a mother look.

A ten-second kaleidoscope of pictures shifted through her mind. Beth holding Hunter at knifepoint, threatening him like a gangster. Beth screaming she knew where the treasure was in an attempt to save Shannon.

Beth snoring like a hibernating bear.

"If that's what the doctor says." A hint of a smile formed on Shannon's lips. "We'll call it quality mother-daughter time."

— 21 —

Shannon shared a hospital room with Beth for a few days because of her own concussion, but they hadn't engaged in much girl talk. Surgeons removed Beth's spleen, ruptured when her captors had kicked her.

Shannon, sitting in her hospital bed, looked up from the fisherman sweater she was knitting. Finally, a healthy pink color had begun to brighten Beth's face, offsetting the greenish violet splotches.

Shannon hoped her mother would sleep awhile. Beth might not like what she had in mind.

Shannon slipped on her quilted robe and padded slowly down the hall to the elevators, trying to ignore her endless assortment of aches and pains and the IV stand she had to maneuver with every step.

She rode to the top floor and walked to a room guarded by a policeman.

"Ma'am, are you lost?" The tall officer stared at her as if he were a school principal.

"I'm not. I have permission to visit this man." Shannon handed him the paperwork she'd obtained by nearly threatening Chief Grayson.

The policeman unlocked the door and stood in the doorway. Shannon walked in.

Lying in bed, wearing two bulky leg casts, Hunter looked

up. Then away.

Michael had told her that Li Chung, annoyed with his flunky, had ordered his legs broken, but horror stirred afresh in Shannon at the sight. She forced her voice to sound casual. "Hello, Hunter."

"Hi." He still didn't meet her gaze.

"May I sit?"

"You can do anything you want. Me …?" He glanced at his casts, at the door the officer had just closed, and shrugged.

Shannon sat on an unpadded gray chair. "I don't feel sorry for you, Hunter."

"You shouldn't." For the first time, he looked at her. Blotches like Beth's marred his perfect tan. "I'm the one who should be sorry. And I am—though I doubt you believe that."

"If I didn't, I might not have come." She looked straight into his eyes, eyes that once had melted her. Now gray-green, they resembled the Simmuem River on a bleak November morning.

"Thanks for not pressing burglary charges on top of—of kidnapping." His shoulders hunched. "I'll go to prison, but my lawyer's trying to work out a deal. If I testify against Chung and Bai, the judge might lighten my sentence."

Still an operator. Hunter would enter a courtroom in a wheelchair, clean-cut and pitiable. He'd work his magic on judge and jury, as he did on everyone. Shannon sighed.

"I *am* sorry, Shannon." Beads of sweat glistened on his forehead. "I met Chung at a maritime history conference, and he seemed like the answer to my lack of funds. I didn't realize he was a—a piranha until too late. When I protested his methods and tried to protect you, he threatened me. Eventually, he made good on his threats." He looked at his legs again.

Protect me? Shannon recalled the feeling of Hunter's gun in her back, saw it pointing at her as she walked into the sea. She stood.

"I know it's hard to believe, but I hated what I did to you. I cared for you very much. I still do." With an effort, he reached for her hand. Shannon noticed he no longer wore his agate ring. A shame. It made a great lie detector.

She stuffed her hands into her pockets. "Hunter, if my grandfather reneged on promises to your grandfather, I'm sorry. But that does not excuse for a minute what you did." She softened her voice. "I do accept your apology. I forgive you."

His face lit for a moment, then fell as she continued, "But after we meet in court, I never want to see you again."

*   *   *

Shannon didn't look back, and she didn't stop until she reached the elevators. *I did it.*

Despite her earlier words, Shannon felt sorry for Hunter, lying helpless in bed, his legs and dreams broken. She truly had forgiven him, but she hadn't caved in to his charisma. Stepping onto the elevator, she mentally waved goodbye and good riddance.

Her tired body cheered her re-entrance to her room. She climbed into bed and debated which should come first: book or nap?

"Did you talk to Hunter?" Beth was looking at her as if she'd missed curfew.

"You knew he was here too?"

"Mothers find out these things." Beth raised the head of her bed and said casually, "Did you clear things up between you?"

"Oh, yes." Shannon grimaced. "I told him we were through forever, and I think he understood me. Loud and clear."

"Smart girl."

"Are you feeling better? I haven't seen you smile like that in days."

"I am. And I'm proud of you, darling." Beth put fingers to her swollen lips and blew Shannon a kiss.

How could I have ever thought she was after the treasure?

"May I ask you something?" Shannon blurted it out before she thought. *Great. Poor Beth's recovering from surgery, and you pester her with questions. Questions that might hurt.*

"I've got time." A faint grin played around Beth's lips. "You too. It's a good time to talk."

Shannon hesitated, then said, "Why didn't Victoria make you her heir instead of me?"

She expected at least a tinge of anger. But Beth simply said, "Because I asked her to."

"You did?"

"Of course." Beth enumerated on her fingers. "First, I needed to stay off radar. Living as a Paisley heiress wouldn't accomplish that, especially with our family links to the Camorra. Second, my mother spent huge sums to ensure my survival, and third, she also set me up in business. I refused to let her give me more. And finally—" Now Beth gave Shannon a sly look. "I hoped that eventually the money, the house, and the shop might bring you to America so I could see you again. And the twins."

"You are one conniving woman." Shannon tried to sound stern.

"I am." Beth's eyes twinkled. "I don't apologize in the least."

A tap on their door interrupted. Shannon frowned. How

many times did the nurses have to prod and poke them? *My blood pressure was fine—until you showed up.*

Instead, Michael's voice disarmed her. "May I come in?"

Her frown flip-flopped. "Of course."

He looked as joyous as a ten-year-old who had hit his first home run. "I had to pull strings to bring these, and we can't keep them long. But here they are—"

He freed a large framed document from its white-sheet wrapping. And held up a doubloon.

Shannon's jaw dropped to her collarbone. She touched its glass with one finger. She held the coin, running her fingers over its engraved surface.

"I assume Li Chung framed the map for you. How nice of him," Michael said. He held it up so Beth could see it too. "Treasure hunt, anyone?"

*   *   *

At last, the coin Hunter had stolen. The images of the cross and lion she'd seen only in Michael's photos. She'd longed to hold it, but now a small, vague something bothered her. Perhaps because Bai had held it too?

Not a Scot, that woman, but definitely a Soaper.

"Want to see the coin?" Shannon handed it to her mother. Michael gave Shannon the map.

"I can't believe you brought this." Shannon turned it over. "Look, it's covered with glass on both sides. I can read the clues on the back, just as Grandfather said in the journal." She squinted at the faded but mostly legible handwriting.

"Chung apparently had it treated with the most current

preservation techniques," Michael said.

"How long can she keep it?" Beth craned her neck. Shannon shifted the map so her mother could see better.

"Only an hour or two. Then it has to go back as evidence," Michael said. "But Chung's computers contained copies of this map and clues I've already sent to your e-mail. I thought they might be helpful."

"Just a little." Shannon threw him a grateful look. "Thank you."

Michael returned a glance that sent a happy shiver up her spine. It radiated through her as she examined the yellowed map, turning it over to examine the clues.

"After picking up bits and pieces from Grandfather's journal, how incredible to see them all listed in a row." She bounced in her hospital bed. "See, here are Angus's references to the Simmuem River, Sidhe Glen, and Black Donald's Hand. His riddle about Parable Rock's more elaborate than the others." She read:

> "'My faither doth call me Prodigall,
> But delicious meat I find my bean-hool.
> Christe Jesus told the story,
> Yet He willna own the doubloon's glory,
> Nor a wee tithe of the treasure near.'

"In his journal, James refers to himself as a prodigal too." Shannon clicked her tongue. An unfortunate likeness to his ancestor.

Michael peered at the clue list. "What's a bean-hool? And what's that got to do with anything?"

"Found in the Bible according to Angus," Shannon said. "Bean hulls. An old Scottish expression. The prodigal son was reduced to eating empty bean pods. Only, Angus liked his 'delicious meat.'"

She frowned. "The 'dark glass' riddle doesn't seem an actual clue." She read:

"Ye see through the glass darkly.
Aye, the devil's son I am—
Yet not so dark ye shouldna ken
Which way is true, which way is sham."

Beth eyed her. "You don't have to figure this out today."

"I guess not." The emotional visit with Hunter, the exhilaration of seeing the map and coin—Shannon almost had forgotten she sat in a hospital bed. She leaned back against her pillow. "Perhaps it's not the best time to work on this." She picked up the map, so heavy in its rich wooden frame, to move it to the night table.

"I almost didn't bring it because I knew you'd try." Michael stooped to take it from her.

"But it is a good time to say thank you." She halted him halfway with a look. "Thanks for saving my life. Again."

"Thank you, Michael." Beth's gratitude echoed softly from the other bed.

He straightened, his eyes on the floor. "If only I hadn't flown to LA the night Banks abducted you—"

"You were supposed to stay in Apple Grove every minute?" Shannon snorted. "If only I hadn't confronted him by myself. Dumb move."

"If we start listing all our 'if onlys,' we'll make ourselves crazy," Beth's sensible mother voice broke in. "I'm much more interested in learning how Michael found us."

Shannon had wondered too. "Tell us, please?"

He raised his shoulders in a slight shrug. "Not as difficult as you'd think. Deborah worried when you and Beth didn't come home. Fortunately, Beth told her where you and Banks had gone. I talked to employees there who described you both, then checked nearby ERs." A muscle worked in his cheek. "I drew the conclusion something was wrong, but it had nothing to do with illness."

You're wrong there. A gun in the back will make anyone sick. Shannon fought a surge of anger, then calmed herself. *You've forgiven Hunter. Don't let him control you.* "How did you find Li Chung's 'cottage'? I'm sure he kept his little retreat top secret."

"True. But after you followed Bai, I put a tail on her too. She visited the cottage twice, and it appeared the logical hideout. I contacted the Portland police, we gathered a SWAT team, and the rest is, thankfully, history."

"Since you're answering questions," Shannon said, "I've wondered how Chung and Hunter knew where to find the secret room."

Michael gave his head a light slap. "I meant to mention that I also e-mailed the blueprints of your house; Chung and Banks had studied them before the burglaries. Apparently, they obtained them from the county museum archives, included in 1930s newspaper accounts when the Paisley mansion's construction was hot news. Chung and Banks had marked three closets on the prints, apparently where they guessed

James might build his secret room."

"Thanks. I think." Shannon shivered. "I'm not sure how they knew it even existed, as Grandfather surely wanted to keep his secret room a secret! But he may have mentioned his intention to build one to Corny—probably when he was drunk."

Michael nodded. "According to Banks, Corny wrote letters to his girlfriend during the war about Captain Paisley and the treasure. He included information the Captain probably would have preferred that he had forgotten."

"Those post-treasure-hunt tavern stops weren't a good idea." Shannon had told Michael about the awful ride in Hunter's car, including when he accused her grandfather of ignoring Corny's starving woman and child. "I wonder if, instead of asking Grandfather for help after the war, Corny's girl didn't—"

"Try to extort money from him?" Michael finished her sentence. "In a word, yes. To the point of accusing him of fathering her child." He took Shannon's hand. "Banks didn't tell that part to the police. I tracked down the girlfriend. She's eighty-five now, with a lifelong history as a pathological liar. Given the fact she raised both Banks and his father, it doesn't surprise me that they saw themselves as victims."

A picture of Hunter floated through Shannon's mind, sitting in a wheelchair, using his broken legs to draw sympathy from a jury. *How sad that families sometimes damage people rather than nurture them.*

She said simply, "Thank you again, Michael."

"You're welcome."

"Yes, thanks for helping our family," Beth added.

She sounds tired. Shannon turned to Beth. She looked

cheerful, but her face had paled behind her bruises. "Are you all right?"

Her mother pshawed. "You look almost as bad as I do."

"Not quite." Their nurse had entered. "But you both need rest."

Shannon grimaced. "OK, but—"

"No buts." The nurse threw a meaningful glance at Michael. "Visit a few minutes more, but you need to take care of yourself if you want the doctor to release you tomorrow, Shannon."

"She's leaving tomorrow?" Beth asked.

"You were asleep when I saw the doctor this morning." The doctor had preferred she stay another day, but Shannon had talked him out of it. "Of course, bossy Deborah won't let me do much, but I can check out Michael's files. Soon I'll be out and about." She hugged herself. "It will be so wonderful to concentrate on the treasure without worrying about burglars or kidnappers—"

"Or Banks?" Michael asked.

Shannon swallowed. His eyes held hers with a wistfulness that made her wish they could talk—alone. She said, "I'm glad he's no longer in the picture."

She was rewarded with a broad Michael smile.

He reached for the doubloon Beth handed him and picked up the map. "I'd better return these to headquarters. Otherwise, you'll start messing with clues again."

Shannon let him take it. "Like that will stop me. You sent me Chung's copies, remember?"

"You really want to access those over public Wi-Fi?"

Um, no. Flushing, she pressed a button and lowered her bed. "Go away. The more I rest, the sooner I'll get out of here. And the sooner I'll find the treasure."

"So you think you'll be able to do it, when generations of your family couldn't?" Michael shot her an insolent grin.

She gave him a thumbs-up. "I think so. With a little—no, lots!—of help from my friends."

Shannon let the last words drift into a question.

He turned, sat on her bed, and raised his thumb beside hers. "We'll find it," Michael said.

At his nearness, she closed her eyes. But her avoidance did no good, because she felt his light kiss on her hair before heavy footsteps told her he'd left the room.

— 22 —

A sea of contentment. An ocean of discontent.

How could Shannon swim in both at the same time?

The artsy pastels of her study had never seemed so exquisite, the fire, so welcoming. She'd thought she would never see this room again, and she snuggled in her grandmother's afghan, sated with gratitude and joy.

Yet she didn't want to be here.

She wanted to search for Parable Rock with the Purls. To follow on Aaron's heels as he and Kate combed the hills for Black Donald's Hand. Most of all, she longed to dig with Michael and the twins in Witch Cave. Lara texted that they now resembled cave dwellers who hadn't yet discovered baths.

Yes, she'd promised her family she'd stay cocooned in this lovely room.

But she had to get out of here.

Slowly she walked to the back stairway.

Deborah stood on the landing. "I knew you couldn't stay put."

Shannon grinned. "Is Beth asleep?"

"Yes, she's resting easier now." Deborah opened the closet door and began shoving coats aside.

"You read my mind." Shannon started to enter.

"Stay out until I'm finished," Deborah shook a finger in her face. "I'm doing it to keep you from doing it. Although I don't know what you think you'll find in there. You've been in that room a zillion times."

Shannon fumed, but she obediently backed out until Deborah gestured her in.

She slid the side panel aside, keyed the complex code into the vault lock, and swung the door open. The papery smell, strong as ever, greeted her. She inhaled before entering, as usual, and sat in the stout oak chair Beth said James preferred. Shannon lit the hurricane lamp and slipped manila folders from the desk. Flicking on her phone, she again ran down the list of Angus's map clues from Michael's files.

Simmuem River
A-twistin' and turnin', chaingin' like a woman,
Whose name it doth bear.
Aye, she's a kelpie stream,
Think to embrace her without care?

Sidhe Glen
Fear all this buriall plaice today,
Gredy ghaisties, gang ye away!
Plundered gold from Francis be mine
Never his, never thine.

Black Donald's Hand
Black Donald holds all the land in his evile grip.
I, his brother, am free to roam.
He laughs at the fair sight of me,
Raises fyngers and olde knaggy thombe.

Parable Rock
My Father doth call me the Prodigall,
But delicious meat I find my bean-hool.

Christe Jesus told the story,
Yet He willna own the doubloon's glory,
Nor a wee tithe of the treasure near.

Wench's Cave
How canna forget the bonnie wench,
Witchy hair fallin' to her knee?
Strong lass a-dancin', soaper a-dancin',
Luve and gowld for me, but death to thee.

Dark Glass
Ye see through the glass darkly.
Aye, the devil's son I am—
Yet not so dark ye shouldna ken
Which way is true, which way is sham.

For the thousandth time, Shannon shuddered at the evil that Angus embraced, thankful that James, at the end of his life, showed regret for his dark obsession. She prayed for a bit, examining her own drive to find the treasure.

Oh, yes, she wanted to find it. Golden coins, a pearl of great price—both stirred her imagination and awakened desire. Yet they destroyed the people who spent all to possess them. The treasure gave them nothing.

She wanted to find it and give it away. Give it away so she, her children, and her future grandchildren would never be lured by its luster. Shannon reviewed the clues with fresh resolve.

Angus's full clues about the river, the burial ground, Black Donald's Hand, and the cave filled in a few holes and demonstrated Angus's poetic talent, but they didn't add much to what she already knew from James's notes. Nor, actually, did the Parable Rock lines.

And the "dark glass" clue? It confused her more than ever. But had James's dismissal of this hint kept him from solving the mystery?

Aaron told her that no large concentrations of obsidian had been found in Smugglers' Cove. Less, actually, than in surrounding areas. Had Angus found one little deposit that pointed to the treasure? She could ponder that till the ocean ran dry.

Instead, Shannon dug in the bookshelves and found the little King James New Testament she'd seen when she first discovered James's logs. She liked to think that toward the end of his life, he had opened it again.

She used the concordance app on her phone to find the verse Beth had suggested: 1 Corinthians 13:12. "For now we see through a glass, darkly; but then face to face: now I know in part; but then shall I know even as also I am known."

Shannon checked a modern version and found the passage referred to a mirror. Of course, first-century mirrors did not reflect clear images; in fact, they often distorted objects they reproduced.

That certainly applied. She'd struggled these past weeks with the constant sense that she had followed clues with accuracy, yet the answers seemed all wrong.

She read them again, slowly. She studied the map until her eyes hurt.

Nothing stood out.

Shannon leafed through Michael's photos of the doubloon. Again, that odd little negative impression she'd experienced when she held the real article while in the hospital, a sensation like a wiggling tadpole. She stared at the pictures again.

Shannon exited the vault-room and closet, and blinking in the brightness, took the photos to her study. She tapped keys on her laptop. Images of antique doubloons rose on the monitor, then an enlarged one of the coin that mirrored James's find.

It *mirrored* James's doubloon.

Shannon leaped from the chair. Pulling out her phone again, she pushed her slow body down the hall toward the back door.

Her phone rang. *Blast.* She didn't want to talk—

Betty. Good.

"We've found Parable Rock! It's a cross, and it's not that far from Witch Cave!" Her friend's voice vibrated with gladness.

Shannon grabbed a coat from a hook, yanked the door open, and headed for the garage. "Betty, would you tell the Purls to meet me at the footbridge—"

"You're *not* coming here today, and that's final." Betty morphed into a mom. "I only told you because I wanted to encourage you."

"I have to come." If only she could walk faster. "Would you call Kate and tell her and the guys to meet me there too? I'll call Michael and have him bring the cave bunch to the bridge—"

"Why? Have you lost your mind?" Betty demanded.

"We need to regroup. I'm sorry, Betty, but I don't think that's Parable Rock."

"*What?*"

"That's why I want to come." Shannon opened the garage and headed for Old Blue. "We've been going about this all wrong."

— 23 —

The dirty, weary group Shannon faced at the footbridge looked as if they'd gladly throw her off it. She'd obviously embarrassed her twins, who slunk to the rear.

Perhaps she should have explored her idea with Michael first.

He cleared his throat. "Maybe you'd like to inform us of this new hypothesis?"

Doubts, like barnacles, tried to suction to her. She shook them off. "I'll be glad to." She held up the largest photo of James's coin and its Internet twin. "I noticed something new. The doubloon James found looks exactly like this one, except that the lion on James's doubloon is on the wrong side of the cross. It's the mirror image of other doubloons of that era."

"You think it's fake?" Alec burst out. Shannon noticed he'd moved to the front of the group.

"We can't know for certain until an antique coin expert examines it," Shannon said, "and that may be awhile, as it's considered evidence in upcoming court trials. But given Angus's clue, I think that coin's genuine, just flawed. He certainly noticed the doubloon's reversed image and used the flaw to confuse other treasure hunters."

"Well, he did a great job. I'm confused." Joyce crossed her arms. "Why did he even bother to make a map?"

"He drew the map with his own interests in mind."

Shannon pulled a copy out of her coat pocket and pointed. "The landmarks Angus indicated would help him find his loot when he returned to Oregon, perhaps years later—but they represented a *mirror image* of the real landmarks and the real site of the treasure in order to protect it." She shifted her finger. "We've been hunting south of the Simmuem. I believe the true landmarks—and the treasure—are located north of the river."

"But what about Parable Rock?" Betty insisted. "The formation we found is distinctive—and well hidden, I must say—and it fits the clue to a T." She gestured across the river. "Do you think there's another cross on that side?"

"Not necessarily. The real Parable Rock may resemble something else. I'm sure, though, that Angus matched the clues to convincing south-side landmarks, as well as north." She held up the Internet photo of the doubloon. "I believe we'll find a doubloon with the right imprint buried near the real Parable Rock."

"But why would he bother to bury a coin there?" Joyce stuck her hands on her hips. "He knew the real landmarks."

"Angus buried the second coin, I think, as an artificial landmark, in case the natural ones changed or disappeared," Shannon answered. "He believed Black Donald held 'all the land in his evile grip.' Who knows? Angus was familiar with the wild coastal weather, and he may have experienced a landslide or even a minor earthquake while he was in Oregon. He also had no idea when he'd return.

"And maybe, just maybe, Angus buried the doubloon as a kind of grudging reward for whoever solved his mirror riddle, confirming she was on the right track." Shannon smiled wryly. "Fits with what Grandfather wrote in his journal about Angus's giving the map to his sons. He said he used his head, and they should use theirs."

Aaron spoke up. "I don't know of any Native American burial grounds north of the river."

Shannon's confidence wavered a bit. "No other cemeteries either," she admitted. "I don't yet know the answer to Sidhe Glen. But I believe this is the way to go. And I don't want you all to keep working so hard for nothing."

Shannon wanted to drop her gaze to the ground to avoid all the penetrating eyes on her. Instead, she raised her chin. "I appreciate you so much. Please feel free to head for Espresso Yourself for coffee and snacks—Essie will be there."

"What are *you* going to do?" Michael, who'd remained silent, stepped forward.

She looked away. "I'm going to look for Parable Rock."

She heard Betty's exasperated sigh. "You're not even supposed to be here."

"I'm feeling better. I have to do this."

"I'll go with you." Michael gently slid his arm around her. "You may need someone to carry you home."

Small fireworks burst inside Shannon, but she retorted, "I think I'll walk on my own two feet, thank you."

He grinned.

"We're going too, Mum." Lara and Alec stepped up.

"Of course, we are," the Purls chorused. Betty shrugged and smiled.

Aaron took Kate's hand. "I wouldn't miss this for anything."

"Thank you." Shannon opened her arms, and they all clasped in a huddle. Michael's powerful arm encircled her shoulders. She leaned against Alec's skinny chest, her own heart thudding like a parade drum.

The grungy group crossed the footbridge and headed north along the shoreline. The twins ran ahead, nosing around clumps of rocks like Irish setters.

Fortunately, the weather cooperated, offering an afternoon of chilly but sun-kissed winds. Michael and Betty made Shannon rest at regular intervals, but the joy of the hunt energized her like no snooze on a sofa could—for an hour. Then the others, too, began to trudge rather than walk. Betty's determined strides wilted to a slow walk. Joyce's perpetual magenta lipstick caked on her straight-line mouth, and she fell several yards behind.

No wonder. They searched for hours before I came. Should she turn the group around?

"It's really a lovely day to be outside." Melanie, at Shannon's elbow, had read her doubts and positioned herself to encourage. Melanie swept the landscape with a slim hand. "I know we're supposed to look at the rocks, but I can't help watching the patterns on the hills when the sun peeks through the clouds."

Shannon followed her gaze, her spirits lifting. Large arcs of sunlight, like smiles, curved on the hillsides. If God was smiling on the earth, how could she do otherwise?

The corners of Betty's mouth drifted downward, however, and she pointed. "That big old tree, though—it almost ruins the ambiance. Looks like something out of a horror movie."

A huge tree protruded from a barren ridge ahead of them, twisted at a grotesque angle. *Must be hundreds of years old.* She'd read about pines like this, stubborn old conifers that survived years of storms, landslides, lightning, disease, and man's axes. Shannon agreed with her friend, though. A thing of beauty it wasn't. A single lifeless limb protruded out of the tree's thick trunk, and only a few gnarly branches of needles spread from the other side of the trunk like—

Like fingers. *Like a hand.*

Trembling, Shannon reread the map clues on her cell.

"Betty, you are incredible!" Shannon threw her arms around her friend.

"Um, thanks." Betty stared at her in bewilderment.

Shannon laughed and called to Michael, who was about to disappear into a fortress of cliffs. He turned and jogged back to them. "What's up?"

Shannon wanted to dance him across the sand, but she gestured toward the tree, then at the clues, and read aloud. "'He laughs at the fair sight of me, Raises fyngers and olde knaggy thombe.'" She whirled Betty in circles and gasped, "I think Betty has spotted Black Donald's Hand. If I'm right, we'll find Parable Rock directly in line with it."

*   *   *

"It's a sheep."

Shannon and the rest of her treasure-hunting crew guffawed at Alec's slack jaw, but she shared his wonder. The wind and waves had carved a bigger-than-life lamb. Reclining on a bed of black basalt and gravel, their art might have competed with a sculptor's efforts.

"Black sheep," Michael commented. "Fits this guy."

"Makes more sense than the cross," Betty admitted. "Jesus told the parable of the lost coin, the lost sheep, and the prodigal son all together to make a point about God's love."

"Both James and Angus considered themselves prodigals," Shannon said. *At least one, I think, made his way home.*

The sun was headed home too, and the tide soon would sweep in. Shannon threw herself into organizing the dig, and everyone, with fresh energy, poked and raked around Parable Rock.

"Mum!" Lara, exploring along the back of the sheep, yelled in delight.

Shannon dashed to her daughter.

"She's dug up something, all right." Alec sounded envious, but he helped Lara push the last shovels of gravelly mud away from a tiny rusty box. Lara handed it to Shannon.

She tugged, but its little lock held. She grasped the box a moment, praying it would lead to the end of this search, then handed it to Michael.

He pulled tools from his kit. "Let's take it where there's more light."

They gathered on a sandy stretch of beach, trying to stay out of Michael's way, yet compelled to inch closer. Shannon held her breath as she watched him work, patiently probing this, jiggling that.

Hurry up! she wanted to scream like a five-year-old. *I want to see now!*

Finally, Michael loosened the lock. The buzz of conversation died. He stood and carried the box to Shannon. The others rose from sand and rocks to gather around her. Alec and Lara held up their phones, ready to take pictures.

Shannon raised the box's squeaky lid—and found a pile of tattered oilcloth. No glimmer of gold met her eyes, and her breath coagulated in her chest.

She probed the cloth and found a single tarnished coin. She held it up, and one of the sun's last rays clutched it in a golden, greedy grasp.

A doubloon with a cross engraved on it, a small lion on the correct side.

— 24 —

"**I** can't believe you went treasure hunting without me." Beth's grin contradicted her accusation.

"I couldn't very well wheel you out there on a gurney." Shannon helped Beth to the sofa nearest the study fireplace, then plopped beside her.

"Call me when you find *the* treasure. I'll come, no matter what."

Shannon sighed. "You'll probably heal before we do that."

Beth rested her hand on Shannon's. "So you think finding the rest of the treasure won't prove as easy."

"When Lara dug up that doubloon, I thought I would fly." For a moment, Shannon relived the thrill of knowing her "mirror" hunch had paid off. "Perhaps success the first day raised my expectations too high. Witch Cave seemed such a nice, defined landmark. James thought so too. Yet I think the word 'witchy' in Angus's clue sent Grandfather in the wrong direction. Angus called it the 'wench' clue." She shook her head. "None of the named caves north of the river seem to relate. If we hadn't found the second doubloon, I'd really wonder if I'd goofed again."

"You haven't." Michael tapped on the door. He carried a tray of steaming mugs. "I stole these from Deborah so you'd let me in."

"You're always welcome." Shannon emphasized "always"

before she thought. Blushing, she quickly focused on his initial words. "You've figured something out?"

"About the treasure's actual location? No." He handed Beth a mug and set the tray on the end table near her. Stirring the right amount of cream and sugar into Shannon's repaired butterfly mug, he handed it to her. "But I might have found Sidhe Glen. I called a friend who owns a detection dog, and we covered the area near Black Donald's Hand. Three hundred yards south of the tree, the dog gave two definite alerts."

"Can a dog smell graves more than 400 years old?" Shannon asked.

Michael nodded as he sat across from her. "This is a historical human remains dog, trained to detect old bones and teeth. Some of these dogs can find ancient graves."

"'Fear all this buriall plaice today,'" Shannon quoted softly. "So Sidhe Glen does exist north of the river."

"Creepy spot," Michael sipped his own tea. "Weird rock formations. Wind moans as it blows through them."

"More like what I'd expected," Shannon said. "The Native American burial ground seemed too beautiful, too serene to fit Angus's clue."

"We reported the possible presence of graves to the state, and when I told them our treasure story, they mentioned sending an anthropologist to the gravesite." Small wrinkles creased Michael's forehead. "I hope this won't turn out to be a mixed blessing. The state antiquities people have expressed great interest too, since we turned in the new doubloon. They may want to join us. And bring their red tape."

"Let them help you dig," Beth smirked. "We'll see how long they stick around."

"I wish they could tell us *where* to dig." Shannon took the laptop from her desk and opened a file. "Aaron gave me a map and a list of geological landmarks north of the river, official and unofficial, including Native American names. Nothing connects with Angus's wench clue."

She printed out copies and handed them to Michael and Beth. "See what you think."

Shannon had mulled them over until she almost could recite them. Kingfisher Rock. Nixíxunu (Tillamook for "Thunderbird") Cave. Double-Keg Cliff. G eclá (Tillamook for "Ice") Point. Suncatcher View. Oluk (Snake) Ridge. Whale-Watchers' Point. Moon Cave.

"Where is this Moon Cave?" The sharpness in Beth's voice startled them.

Shannon said, "Looks less than a quarter mile from Parable Rock. But then, so are Double-Keg Cliff and G eclá Point."

"Perhaps I'm making too much of the Soaper clue." Beth planed her voice to normalcy. "But they carried out many of their evil activities according to the phases of the moon."

Yes. Shannon could see Angus's witchy-haired Soaper wife dancing madly in the moonlight, luring her next victim to his death.

She turned to Michael. "I'd like to see Moon Cave."

*   *   *

They had wanted to scout the cave, just the two of them. But Shannon simply had to ask Aaron if he thought past earthquakes had raised the cave above sea level. Kate gleaned the information from Aaron and told the other

Purls. When Shannon and Michael realized an entourage would accompany them, she called the twins to join in the fun.

Michael notified the State Historic Preservation Office, which planned to send Henry Hartford to oversee the dig.

"They like the idea of our finding a fabulous treasure and turning it all over to them," Michael told Shannon.

"I hope we can work together." Shannon had heard the SHPO took its preservation role very seriously. Her concerns multiplied when the agency mailed her pounds of paperwork to read and sign.

Henry, a small, sandy-haired man, seemed pleasant enough, but as they gathered on the beach, he confirmed he would take charge.

"Let's make it our goal to disturb the cave as little as possible," he said. "I like the idea of using skewers to explore. Also, use your clam rakes rather than shovels. We can't destroy Moon Cave to find this treasure. Please follow these rules, or I'll have to stop the dig."

Shannon gritted her teeth, and she saw Michael's lips tighten. *Neither of us likes to take orders. No wonder we sometimes cross swords.*

On the other hand, Henry had made a valid point: A group this size could cause irreparable damage. Not only would that harm the environment, but the Preservation Office might shut down the operation permanently.

That possibility hadn't seemed real before ....

Henry's speech quieted everyone on the short trek from a parking lot to the cave, but it couldn't dispel the carnival atmosphere completely. Joyce handed out cupcakes topped with gold-wrapped chocolate coins, proclaiming, "A cupcake for every occasion and an occasion for every cupcake."

"Oh, yeah." Alec wolfed down several.

The coast basked in sunshine, trying to pretend winter would bypass them. Shannon almost regretted leaving the warmth and blue sky outside to work in Moon Cave. But when they arrived at the cliff that concealed its surprisingly large mouth, she could hardly wait to begin.

"Glad we don't have to scuba dive." Aaron shivered, looking at the innocent-looking, icy waves that lapped the shore. "Angus probably had to swim, maybe make a couple of trips, to hide his treasure. The cave entrance remained at least partially submerged, even at low tide, until the 1700 earthquakes raised it."

The treasure hunters carried gear down a narrower passage into a large main cavern. A hole in the ceiling made Moon Cave less forbidding than Witch Cave.

"The moon shines in at night," Henry said. "You've never seen anything so beautiful, so mysterious."

His tone told Shannon he loved the land and water. *Maybe he's not so bad.*

Everyone chose an area to explore, flashlight beams bouncing off rock walls. Despite her claustrophobia, Shannon selected a small niche in the back of the main cavern. She poked, scraped, and raked near the cave's floor, adding her percussion to the symphony of discovery around her. She and the Purls chatted as they worked. She listened to Aaron's stories about the Tillamook and the Nehalem, both tribes in the area. His Tale of the South Wind engrossed her so much that she almost didn't hear the small clang of her metal skewer on metal.

"Find a pork-and-beans can too?" Alec kidded her. He'd taken plenty of ribbing when he unearthed a false alarm.

"I'll help." Michael moved from his site to Shannon's. She didn't need his assistance, but to her surprise, she appreciated the gentlemanly gesture. Her appreciation grew the more they scraped. And raked. And scraped.

"Are these scraps of cloth?" Shannon poked dark shreds scattered throughout the rocky earth.

Michael thrust several handfuls into a plastic bag from his kit. "Might be interesting to have them analyzed."

That metallic sound again. And again.

"There's something here." Michael said it when Shannon's astonished mind couldn't grasp the words.

The others gathered around them like gulls. Shannon glanced at Henry from time to time. His sandy eyebrows seemed permanently raised, his mouth hanging slightly open. *Please don't manufacture a reason to stop us.*

A chest. Shannon rubbed her eyes.

Michael slowly edged the rusty metal chest, the size of a small microwave, from its recess. "Don't try to move that," he said.

"It's not that big." Shannon tugged on it anyway. The chest didn't budge. "Whoa."

Michael rolled his eyes, but drew tools from his bag and began to work the heavy lock.

Shannon ran to the cave entrance so she could get cellphone reception and called her mother. "Hello, Beth? We've found something."

"We're on our way." Beth hung up before Shannon could say more.

She returned to the group surrounding Michael. Everyone,

including Henry, stood in silence. Shannon inhaled the fishy, salty smell of the cave, watched shadows flicker on the others' faces, and wondered if her grandfather had ever ventured into this cave. Minutes slogged by, slower, slower, slower ....

The lock dropped. *Clunk.*

Shannon didn't move toward the chest. "Let's wait for Beth."

The others shifted a little restlessly, but she saw agreement in their eyes.

"Of course, we'll wait for your mom," Betty nodded emphatically. "She's been a big part of this."

Shannon had been lingering only a few minutes by the cave entrance when her mother, leaning on Deborah, appeared.

Shannon ran to them. "Are you sure you're OK?"

"Don't fuss over me." Beth continued her beeline to the cave entrance. "Let's see what you found!"

Applause and a celebratory buzz met them in the main cavern.

"Michael's unlocked the chest." Shannon gestured to Beth. "You open it."

"After what you've gone through to find it?" Beth put her hands behind her back. "I certainly will not."

Michael took both their hands. "Open it together."

Shannon glanced at Henry. Michael hadn't asked Henry's permission, but then, Henry, who was half Michael's size, hadn't insisted on it either. "Let's do it."

"Go, Mum! Go, Gram!" Alec pumped his fist.

The glow on Beth's face brightened the cave. She jiggled the latch. Shannon shifted the top of the chest to loosen it, and it opened.

Another tattered oilcloth covering, with its pungent odor. When Shannon pulled the cloth away, she saw gold.

Beth stared. Their fellow treasure hunters gulped a simultaneous, astonished breath. Nobody exhaled.

Dozens of tarnished doubloons sent their best glimmers to greet the watching world. Several ragged velvet bags lay among them. Shannon opened one the color of claret and gently poured its contents into her hand.

Diamonds, glittering like snow on the mountains. Real. She was sure of it.

She handed another wine-colored bag to Beth. Cherry fires glowed in her mother's palm, mixed with jewels the color of glistening leaves.

Beth breathed, "I've never seen this many jewels in my entire life."

Feeling like she'd found Ali Baba's treasure cave, Shannon rippled her fingers through the doubloons. She dug deep and let them clink slowly back into the chest.

Beth replaced the claret bag with a purple one, and a simultaneous, soft "Ohhhh" swept the cave, whispered in its nooks and crannies. She held up a tarnished golden monkey, about four inches long, that wore a robe of sapphires and rubies. He clasped an enormous translucent pearl, as if ready to toss it like a ball. Shannon couldn't take her eyes off the brooch. For this, Li Chung had risked everything.

Now he sat in prison. Hunter did too.

Despite the treasure's beauty and value, was it worth all that? Shannon drew back.

Beth seemed to read her mind. "Thank God, we found it!" she exclaimed. "Now we can forget about this business forever."

"You mean you don't want to do this, Gram?" Lara,

at Beth's elbow, poured doubloons over her grandmother's other hand like water.

"I didn't say that."

Amid the laughter, Shannon said to the others, "You've always wanted to play the part of Ali Baba, right? Or a king or queen? Now you can."

Lara whooped and grabbed one of the velvet bags. "A handful of jewels," she marveled, her eyes glittering like the emeralds she fingered. "I thought, only in my dreams."

"Keep 'em in your dreams," Alec said. "Starving actresses don't rake in this kind of loot."

Shannon noticed, though, that he took his time, trying to look scholarly as he examined them and all but bit a coin.

Thank You, God, that we're giving this away.

While the others took a turn and took pictures, Michael, holding the bag of earth and scraps, drew Shannon aside. "I can't swear to it, but I'm guessing these are from some article of clothing, maybe bloodstained. Given your ancestor's leanings, I wouldn't be surprised if he kept up the good old pirate tradition of burying treasure with blood."

Shannon gulped. "And who would he have victimized? Some-one who knew he'd stolen Drake's treasure. Fits with the Sidhe Glen riddle." She showed the poem on her phone to Michael.

Fear all this buriall plaice today,
Gredy ghaisties, gang ye away!
Plundered gold from Francis be mine
Never his, never thine.

She shuddered. "Perhaps Angus killed and buried him—

or them!—secretly in the hills, then sneaked the shirt down here."

Such awful imaginings seemed worlds away from the fun the Purls enjoyed as momentary royalty. Even level-headed Betty's face lit with wonder as she tried to estimate the number of coins. Joyce shook bags of jewels like maracas as she cavorted to her favorite oldie, "Dancing Queen."

"I've supervised dozens of so-called treasure digs. I—I had no idea ..." Henry, looking dazed, edged closer to the cave entrance, one eye on the chest. Shannon heard him shout into his cell, requesting security measures.

Even Henry took a "treasure turn" when he returned, holding coins with as much amazement in his face as if they had bloomed in his hand.

Security officers arrived soon afterward. Their eyes popped at the sight of the chest, but they carried it out.

"Thanks for your unbelievable honesty and generosity," Henry clasped Shannon's hand. "When we've processed all this, the SHPO will likely host a celebration. We hope you'll attend."

"Let us know." Shannon smiled. "We like celebrations—in case, you couldn't tell."

Henry laughed and hurried out of the cave.

Shannon leaned against the damp, crumbly wall. Her muscles had turned to mush.

"You're done." Deborah took her arm and tugged on Beth's. "You too."

Shannon halted and looked back.

"Don't even think about it," Betty said. "We'll restore any rough areas and gather the tools—"

"Don't worry, Mum." Alec's voice deepened. "We'll take care of it."

Given the walk to the parking lot, she'd let them. They left the cave, blinking in the mild sunlight. Shannon slipped her arm from Deborah's and took Beth's free one. Black Donald's Hand reached from the hill as if to seize them.

"You do not hold all the land in your 'evile grip.'" Shannon thumbed her nose at the specter of a tree.

Beth laughed, Deborah shook her head, and they strolled toward the parking lot and home.

— Epilogue —

Shannon had practiced her speech for the Maritime Museum dinner a hundred times, but the 101st rehearsal looped through her mind as she dipped her spoon into exquisite raspberry mousse.

Chill, Shannon. This isn't a State of the Union address. Only Michael, looking James Bond-ish in his tux, would know if she made a fool of herself. Professional that he was, he wouldn't tell.

When the invitation had arrived, allowing Shannon only one guest, she'd vacillated, even considered refusing. However, when Beth discovered Shannon's dilemma, her mother had insisted she invite Michael. "We owe him our lives."

Now, though she missed her mother, children, and the other treasure hunters at their table, Michael's calm presence meant so much. He'd helped her survive before. He'd help her survive tonight.

When the master of ceremonies called her name, she actually enjoyed the Miss America-like walk to the podium, wearing the slim blue gown she'd beaded for the occasion. Listening to the emcee babble on about her generosity grew a bit tedious. But when the applause quieted and she walked to the microphone, she didn't find it hard to smile. "Thank you so much for a marvelous evening."

The spotlight sucked the next words of her speech from her brain. She realized she'd left her notes in the ladies' room.

For a moment, Shannon existed in emptiness worse than a sci-fi vacuum.

Then brilliant words flooded the back of her throat, but they caught on her tonsils and never made it out of her mouth.

To her surprise, the emcee, standing in the right wing, wore a face-wide grin instead of a grimace. She followed his gaze to a surprise cavalry. Lara, Alec, Beth, the Purls, and Deborah mounted the stage from the left. Michael brought up the rear, his grin wicked and wonderful.

"Ah … uh …" Shannon tried again. "Um …."

Lara, looking like a New York model, slipped her arm around Shannon and spoke into the mic. "I think what my mother means to say is that she wants me to give the speech."

Shannon nodded and hugged her as their audience roared with delight. Lara wowed them with her wit in accepting her mother's appreciation gift from the State of Oregon: a beautiful choker necklace made from Angus's second doubloon, the one she'd uncovered at the real Parable Rock. Her listeners cheered again when Beth clasped it around Shannon's neck.

Standing next to Michael in the background as the emcee claimed the last word, her tongue finally untangled. She whispered to him, "I can't believe I messed up my speech like that."

He touched her hand, then the doubloon on her necklace. "I'll never tell."

Learn more about Annie's fiction books at

AnniesFiction.com

- Access your e-books
- Discover exciting new series
- Read sample chapters
- Watch video book trailers
- Share your feedback

We've designed the Annie's Fiction website especially for you!

Plus, manage your account online!

- Check your account status
- Make payments online
- Update your address

Visit us at AnniesFiction.com

Enjoy this exclusive preview of the
next mystery in the
Creative Woman Mysteries series.

A Tangled Yarn

COMING SOON!

— 1 —

Shannon McClain felt an electric energy fill her craft shop even though Kate Ellis was absent for the weekly meeting. Gathering with the Purls of Hope knitting group on Monday evenings was something Shannon always looked forward to.

"I was hoping Kate would be here." Betty Russo frowned slightly. "I brought in some bones for her dogs." Betty owned The Apple Grove Inn with her husband, Tom, and had a ready supply of dog bones from their inn's kitchen. "She didn't tell me she wouldn't be here tonight."

"She called about fifteen minutes ago. Dog emergency," Shannon said. Kate ran a dog grooming business, Ultimutt Grooming, which was growing in size and in the number of services she provided. "A frantic customer with a sick sheltie had a can't-miss business engagement, and she needed Kate to take her pup to the vet."

Betty nodded and turned to join the other two Purls, Melanie Burkhart and Joyce Buchanan, who were in high spirits. Melanie appeared to be exceptionally cheerful. Her dark-rimmed glasses couldn't hide the sparkle in her green eyes as her excitable chatter added another layer of brightness to the group's usual banter.

Shannon smiled fondly at the table of women collectively known as the Purls. She would always have a special place in her heart for her native Scotland, where she grew up, married, and raised her children. She had, however, grown up not knowing her mother or her maternal grandparents because of a deadly secret that had forced a long, painful separation from them. But now, thanks to the treasured inheritance of the Paisley Craft Market & Artist Loft shop and a grand historic home from her grandmother, she found herself living in Apple Grove, Oregon. Her twin children now attended a nearby university, and she had reunited with her mother. *Life has a way of surprising us now and then*, she thought.

Lighthearted conversation swirled around her as each Purl shared her week and started to focus on her individual project. Just like metal tempered in the fire, all they had gone through together had strengthened their friendship. Shannon was confident nothing could challenge their undying sense of unity.

Shannon pulled out a vibrant green scarf of fuzzy mohair and an unfinished matching hat, a set she was knitting for her daughter, Lara. "Unfinished" was the operative word. At the moment, the hat was merely one inch of completed band spread over circular needles. The dominant color would complement her daughter's eyes, while the texture would add a soft feminine touch.

Finally, as if not able to contain herself any longer, Melanie flicked back her lustrous dark curls, dropped her knitting, and announced, "I went to a fabulous shop in Portland yesterday. It's called Just Knits."

Her enthusiasm not only added a blush to her cheeks but vitality to her movements. A scant two years earlier, the group had been established to assist Melanie emotionally and monetarily as she struggled with breast cancer. Since then they remained a tight-knit group and continued to contribute to other worthy causes. In fact, they met weekly to share in knitting projects and called themselves the Purls of Hope because of this charitable work. It gave Shannon a sense of satisfaction that after she moved here and took over her grandmother's craft store, they continued this tradition by meeting in her shop. Now the Purls were the keystone in her new life, people she could count on in every way.

Betty grinned. "We already have a fabulous knit shop in Apple Grove, and you're in it. Are you saying Just Knits is better than this?" She waved a hand in an arch in front of her, indicating the shop and its walls of books, yarns, beads, tools, and crafting materials for every kind of project, no matter how simple or complex.

"Oh, it's not a knit shop. It sells knitted clothing and afghans. The fabrics are delicious."

"Can we eat them?" Joyce tossed her platinum-blond hair. "Are you saying I have competition now?"

"No." Melanie smiled back at her. "Your bakery is number one for me, hands down. No one can make desserts better than you. But you should feel those things. They're like the proverbial butter melting in your hands."

"Mouth," Betty corrected.

"Whatever," Melanie said, undaunted in her enthusiasm.

"You're making me hungry with all your analogies." Betty's blue eyes twinkled with mischief as she plucked a shortbread cookie off the plate Shannon had strategically placed in the center of the table. "So, did you say this was food or clothing?"

Melanie wrinkled her nose at Betty. "Clothing. It's fabulous—

knitted with yarn made of baby alpaca fiber. You can't believe its downy softness. You just want to pet it." They all chuckled at this image. "I'm serious," she said, smiling. "Warm too. And every item is designed by the owner and handmade."

"What did you get, a sweater or an afghan?" Shannon asked.

Melanie grimaced and shook her head sharply, causing her curls to spring loose and dance around her face. "Neither. Although they were extraordinary and beautiful, they were also extremely expensive. Beyond my means." She paused and then added dramatically, "But I have a plan you'll all love."

"So give." Joyce laughed. "What's your scheme?"

"Well, I thought if Shannon ordered some of those wonderful alpaca yarns for us, we could knit some incredible pieces too. Remember," she said, looking around with a twinkle in her eye, "the Leukemia Society fundraiser is coming up, and we need a special project for it. Maybe Shannon will design hat and scarf sets and some vests for us to knit, and we can donate them to the silent auction. This project should add significantly to the money raised in the auction for cancer research."

Without missing a beat, the group embraced her suggestion and all started talking at once. In the midst of their animated discussion, Shannon said, "Why don't we take an excursion to Portland to see the alpaca pieces and learn more about the yarn? I've read that alpaca yarn doesn't behave the same way wool does when knitted. I'd love to get some tips and pointers from the Just Knits designer."

The response was unanimous. Eager comments flew around the shop. "What a wonderful idea." "It'd be fun." "That's what I was hoping you'd suggest."

The Purls agreed to drive to the city Wednesday and talk with the shop's owner. Although in the middle of the week, the idea of visiting the store and setting up a new project was too exciting to put off. Joyce volunteered her van, allowing the five friends to travel together in comfort.

On Wednesday, however, when they all met at the Paisley Craft Market, they found Kate had left Shannon a message on the shop's phone: she couldn't join them. Duty called, again. One of her best customers had to have her dogs' coats in top shape for a dog show. Time was of the essence.

When Shannon told the others, Betty shook her head and said, "Why didn't she call your cellphone and tell you directly? Leaving a message on your shop's phone when she knows it's not open yet seems odd."

Shannon suspected Betty was miffed because she had always had a close relationship with Kate and was hurt that Kate hadn't called her about the change in plans. Pulling her phone out of her pocket, Shannon examined it. The phone was turned off. "Oh, I forgot. I turned it off earlier when I was at the library. I guess I forgot to turn it back on again." She perused the messages: there, among a couple of others, was one from Kate. She frowned. "Looks like she tried to contact me but couldn't."

Betty seemed relieved. "Good. I was beginning to think she was trying to avoid us."

The others shook their heads.

"Work is work," Joyce said. "She's trying to build her dog business. It takes a lot of time. Don't worry; she'll always be a member of the Purls. We are the five musketeers!" She threw her right arm high into the air, striking a dramatic pose.

Betty grinned at her antics, seemed about to say something, changed her mind, and chuckled again.

As the Purls left the shop and approached the Pink Sprinkles Bakery van, Shannon noticed Joyce hesitate before she moved to the driver's door. She was a good driver, but Shannon knew she didn't relish the hustle and bustle of city driving.

"Would you mind if I drive today?" Shannon asked.

The words had barely cleared her lips when Joyce tossed the keys to her and jumped into the front passenger's seat. Betty and Melanie took the middle seats. The van's yeasty, sweet fragrances filled them with a sense of delight. This would be a fun trip.

"Onward, chariot driver!" Joyce called out with glee and gestured toward the windshield. Her rows of bangles flew down her arm, clicking loudly as they abruptly stopped at her outstretched thumb.

"As you will," Shannon replied, starting the engine and setting off toward Portland.

When they reached the city and exited the highway, Melanie gave directions to Just Knits. "There it is. The one next to the travel agency."

A small, charming shop sat between two contemporary buildings. The boutique mimicked Tudor-style architecture with its half-timbered front and herringbone brickwork— definitely out of a street scene from Charles Dickens's *A Christmas Carol*. Its mullioned bay windows stood out on either side of a heavily carved entrance. In one window, a mannequin wore a multicolored sweater and matching knitted skirt; in the second, afghans in royal blue, logan green, and cinnamon bronze lay draped over a small settee.

A chime rang out as they entered; a tall, lithe woman standing on a ladder and straightening folded items on a high shelf glanced over her shoulder and toward the door.

"I'll be right with you," she called out through the melodious sounds of panpipes and strumming guitars. With a nod and a genial smile she started down the steps.

"We're looking for the designer of these fabulous clothes," Shannon said as the women stepped up to tables piled high with sweaters, some with classic Fair Isle multicolored patterns and others covered with swaths of brightly hued swirls. A child's crayon box couldn't have held more sumptuous colors.

"That would be me. Name's Frances Oberheimer." She smiled again as she introduced herself. "I'm also the owner of Just Knits. Is this your first time here?"

"Yes. Well, except for Melanie," Shannon said.

A look of recognition crossed Frances's face as Melanie stepped forward. "Of course. Hi. I recognize you from the other day."

"I brought my friends with me this time." Melanie absently ran her hand over the pile of sweaters. "I wanted them to see your work."

The woman beamed and gestured around the room. "There's a lot to see. I've increased the number of items I normally carry."

"These are beautiful," Betty gushed as she caressed an argyle sweater she had unfolded on a display table near her. "The design is lovely and the knitting perfect."

"Thank you. I have a professional and talented group of women working for me to produce these. You won't find better anywhere."

For a while the Purls wandered among the tables and shelves admiring, touching, and discussing the various knits. Betty picked out a variegated blue afghan for guests to use in the sitting room at The Apple Grove Inn on cool nights. Joyce chose a conservative argyle sweater in muted tones for her husband, Bill, manager of their local bank. Shannon thought about getting a couple of sweaters for the twins but decided they would be too warm; a vest would be better suited to the climate. Unfortunately, she didn't see any vests.

After a bit, Shannon and the others came up to the desk with their items.

"Melanie was here earlier and she was so excited about your alpaca knits that she wanted us to see your work and learn more about it. We're all knitters and would like to do a series of specialty knits for the Leukemia Society's annual fundraiser. Melanie convinced us to create works made from alpaca. But, before we do, we wanted to talk to you about using alpaca yarn to make hats and scarves for the charity auction. For instance, what are its strengths and weaknesses as a yarn? How does it compare with wool?"

Shannon went on even as Frances turned and started moving away from her. "Since it doesn't have much springiness in its yarn, is it better to use alpaca mixed with wool or maybe design something accenting its different qualities, like more drape and less bounce? So many questions." She smiled ruefully. "We were hoping you could tell us about designing and knitting with it."

Frances faced Shannon. Gone was the warm, friendly shopkeeper, replaced by a frowning, annoyed stranger. She reacted to Shannon's request as if a cold burst of arctic air had come through the room. Her eyes narrowed as she scanned the four women in front of her. "There isn't much to tell. I'm sure you can figure it out."

Her cool attitude surprised Shannon. In her experience, knitters loved to share their knowledge and tips. They were a generous group, as were most crafters. She flashed an appraising glance at Frances. What had set her off? What was her problem?

Betty, who was skillful in working with petulant guests at her inn, also picked up on the note of irritation in Frances's voice. "We thought because you did such beautiful work and obviously were an expert in using alpaca, you might be able to offer guidance." She bestowed her friendliest and most ingratiating smile on her.

Before Frances could respond, however, a petite young woman came into the store. She wore a simple dark skirt and a pink, button-up blouse. Her hair was pulled away from her latte-colored features and gathered into a long, thick black braid. In each of her hands, she clutched the handles of a bulging shopping bag. Seeing so many people, she paused, glancing around with uncertainty.

Frances abruptly announced to the group, "I'm afraid I'm busy and can't chat with you any longer. Please see the clerk about your purchases." Without pausing, she stepped away and summarily flicked her hand toward the newly arrived woman. Frances didn't wait for a reply before striding through a service door at the back of the store. Head down, eyes on the floor, the small woman followed.

"Well," Joyce grumbled as she watched them leave. "Who put the sour in her milk?"

Shannon agreed, but hoped Frances didn't hear her friend's acerbic remark.

Disappointed, but still enamored with their treasures, they silently finished purchasing them and returned to the van.

"What do you think?" Shannon asked.

"So rude." "Certainly not customer friendly." "Needs to learn more about running a business and handling customers." The comments came fast and furious.

"No. No." Shannon laughed. "Not Frances's behavior, although I completely agree with you on that. What about using alpaca yarns to make items for the Leukemia Society's fundraiser? Or would you rather develop a different project for them?"

"After having a second look at the fabrics, I think we should do this even more now," Melanie said, determination reflected in her eyes.

"I agree," Joyce and Betty said in unison.

Shannon nodded. "Yeah. The alpaca drapes differently than sheep's wool, but we can work with that after a little experimentation. I've already checked online and found a couple of places that wholesale quality alpaca yarn. This project is more than doable. Melanie is right; our alpaca knits have a good chance of bringing in quite a bit at the auction."

For the next several miles, the car was filled with the Purls' excited discussion about their newest project.

In the midst of the cheerful plans, Poirot's theme song played on Shannon's cellphone—Lara's ring tone. It was impossible for Shannon to resist a call from her children. Grinning, she noted they were on a quiet stretch of road with few cars about, so she took the call. The others fell silent.

"Greetings, my mysterious daughter," Shannon said, playing on Lara's love of the Agatha Christie novels, "I'm with the Purls. We've been to Portland and are now on the road back to Apple Grove."

"What are you doing? Are you all shopping when you should be working?" Lara teased.

"Wait until you hear about our newest project." Shannon launched into a description of their trip to Portland and Just Knits. She knew Lara would be interested since she shared her mother's creative side and enjoyed handcrafts. She told her daughter about the boutique's unique fabrics produced from handspun, exotic yarns. "As soon I get alpaca yarns into Paisley Craft Market, we'll knit our own pieces for the Leukemia Society."

"Will the Purls use your designs?" Lara asked.

"So far, that's the plan."

Lara giggled. "I knew it. You do the best designs." Predictably, Lara picked up on the energy and spirit of the group and started tossing out ideas. "What about using traditional Pict designs, or at least some Celtic motifs, using tan over dark chocolate?"

Shannon laughed at her daughter's enthusiasm. "Too bad it isn't summer. You could join the fun."

"Don't forget my roommate Patsy's parents, Mr. and Mrs. Barlow, have a fiber farm and it's not too far from Apple Grove," Lara reminded Shannon. "And you wouldn't believe how cute those alpacas and llamas are, Mum. Patsy has these fabulous pictures of them on her wall. So charming!"

"Charming?" Shannon asked with mock skepticism.

"You know what I mean. They are so cuddly. Well, at least the alpacas are—small and unbelievably fluffy. Until they get shorn. Then they look half their original size, but they're still cute!"

"OK, I understand. They're cute."

The Purls couldn't resist grinning at Lara's exuberance.

"Best of all, Patsy told me her mother spins fabulous yarns for local knitters. You and your friends should go over to their farm and see for yourselves. Maybe you could purchase yarns there for your store."

Shannon glanced quickly into the rearview mirror; her friends were nodding back at her. Joyce enthusiastically gave two thumbs-up, the cluster of bejeweled bracelets encircling her wrists chiming merrily.

"Looks like we'll have to visit their farm. I'll phone you for the address after we get home."

"I'll tell Patsy. This is exciting. I wish I could go with you, but I have a big exam coming up and have to study."

"Don't worry, if we buy yarn from her, we'll certainly be going out there again." With that, Shannon said goodbye and dropped the phone onto the console.

Immediately, each of the women started matching their work schedules to be able to go out to see the alpacas together. As they planned, they had no idea what else awaited them at the farm.